SUNRISE

ALSO BY ERIKA KOBAYASHI

Trinity, Trinity, Trinity

SUNRISE

RADIANT
STORIES

ERIKA
KOBAYASHI

TRANSLATED BY BRIAN BERGSTROM

ASTRA HOUSE
NEW YORK

Cover art: *In My Hand—The Fire of Prometheus*, 2019,
C-print 43.2cmx35.6cm (each, set of 3), from the collection of the
artist © Erika Kobayashi. Courtesy of Yutaka Kikutake Gallery.
Photograph by Kasane Nogawa.

For information about permission to reproduce selections from this book,
please contact permissions@astrahouse.com.

Astra House
A Division of Astra Publishing House
astrahouse.com
Printed in Canada

Library of Congress Cataloging-in-Publication Data

Names: Kobayashi, Erika, 1978- author. | Bergstrom, Brian, translator.
Title: Sunrise : radiant stories / Erika Kobayashi ; translated by Brian Bergstrom.
Description: First edition. | New York : Astra House, 2023. |
Summary: "Sunrise is a collection of interconnected stories examining the effects
of nuclear power on generations of women. Connecting changes to everyday life
to the development of the atomic bomb, Sunrise shows us how the discovery
of radioactive power has shaped our history and continues to shape
our future"-- Provided by publisher.
Identifiers: LCCN 2023001043 (print) | LCCN 2023001044 (ebook) |
ISBN 9781662601170 (hardcover) | ISBN 9781662601125 (ebook)
Subjects: LCSH: Kobayashi, Erika, 1978---Translations into English. |
LCGFT: Short stories. | Novellas.
Classification: LCC PL872.5.O245 S86 2023 (print) | LCC PL872.5.O245 (ebook) |
DDC 895.63/6--dc23/eng20230329
LC record available at https://lccn.loc.gov/2023001043
LC ebook record available at https://lccn.loc.gov/2023001044

First edition
10 9 8 7 6 5 4 3 2 1

Design by Richard Oriolo.
The text is set in Adobe Caslon Pro.
The titles are set in BN Tillsdale.

CONTENTS

SUNRISE

SUNRISE

SHE SLOWLY OPENS her eyes. She looks into the light of the sun. The sun is 1,400,000 kilometers in diameter. The energy from the nuclear fusion at its center takes over a million years to reach the surface. The surface heat is over 6000°C. The heat is accompanied by light, light that takes eight minutes and nineteen seconds to reach Earth.

She was born in Tokyo on August 10, two years and a day after Nagasaki was blasted, three days after Hiroshima, by the flash of a nuclear bomb.

She emerged from her mother's womb after ten months and ten days.

She was named Yōko, the *yō* from *Taiheiyō*, Japanese for *Pacific Ocean*.

When she was six years old, she entered elementary school. Her mother divided her long black hair into thirds and braided it. Out in the Pacific, bright light flashed over the Bikini Atoll. The United States was testing bombs, setting them off to see what would happen, atomic first and then hydrogen. A blast of light, a column of water, a mushroom-shaped cloud, out there in the middle of the ocean. The blast washed over a fishing boat, SS *Lucky Dragon No. 5*. Its crew fell ill, and its tuna, now "atomic," was taken to the Tsukiji Fish Market only to be buried in the ground.

She sat beside her mother in the darkness of a movie theater and watched the story unfold as a black-and-white newsreel. Her mother was knitting beside her in the darkness, her fingers as nimble with yarn as with her daughter's hair, and she completed the scarf she was making that very day.

Later that March, the Parliament approved, for the first time since the war, funding for nuclear power. The funding totaled 235 million yen, and production began in earnest to make isotope U-235.

When she was eleven years old, a year before she entered middle school, Japan issued its first 10,000-yen note. It featured Prince Shōtoku, known in ancient times as the Heavenly-being-from-whence-the-sun-rises. She gazed upon his face, enraptured. *Some-*

day I will hold in my hands as many of these as it's possible to hold, she thought.

When she was sixteen years old, she was a senior in high school, and Japan produced its first nuclear-generated electricity. Criticality was achieved in a little village called Tōkai, home of the Japan Power Demonstration Reactor. It made the television news, but her family didn't own a television and she missed it. What she remembers is her middle-school math teacher leaving for Tōkai when her husband got a new job there.

When she was eighteen years old, she went to a women's junior college. Student protests over the US-Japan Security Treaty reached their height, but she remained untouched. She graduated with no trouble and looked for a job.

When she was twenty years old, she got that job, at the Long-Term Credit Bank of Japan. Her hair was no longer divided in thirds and braided—it was short and curled into a permanent wave.

Her wish came true at last: every day, her hands were filled with 10,000-yen notes. They were the bank's, not hers, of course, but she nonetheless lost herself in their count. These days, machines do the counting, but back then it was done by women sitting at windows in banks.

When she was thirty years old, having worked for ten years, she married a man who'd quit being a doctor to pursue his dream of becoming a writer. She herself, soon enough, became the mother of four daughters. I should probably mention that the fourth of these daughters was me. For this is the story of my mother.

Nuclear plants sprang up all over Japan. By the time my mother turned forty, thirty-five reactors delivered 27,881,000 kilowatts of electricity to cities across the country. Their streets glowed day and night with nuclear-powered light.

When she was fifty-one years old, the Long-Term Credit Bank of Japan went under; Yōko's daughters, myself included, had all left home for work or marriage. Yukichi Fukuzawa had long since replaced Prince Shōtoku on the 10,000-yen note. The bank stocks she'd bought with her savings became worth no more than the paper they were printed on.

When she was sixty-three years old, her husband died, followed by her mother the next year. We all had to buy new clothes for each funeral.

The same year her mother died, an earthquake and tsunami struck Tōhoku. The Fukushima Daiichi Nuclear Power Plant exploded in a blast of light. White clouds rose into the sky in internet videos as invisible radioactive material rained down in real life. Her mother's death wasn't due to disaster or radiation, though; it was simply old age. She died at night, on Christmas. She left behind an unfinished sweater and hat and some balls of vivid red yarn. Streetlights and neon signs glowed as snow drifted down from the oddly bright Tokyo night sky.

She wore a brand-new, pitch-black mourning dress with her

hair pulled back and sunglasses on as she counted the money she owed the funeral parlor. Her hands were filled with 10,000-yen notes. Cataract surgery a few years back made even indoor light too bright, and she needed dark glasses to see.

Soon after, we all went to a café. In the background, the Glenn Miller Orchestra played "Moonlight Serenade." I later learned that the song on the original record's B-side was called "Sunrise Serenade."

I also learned that as the world's first nuclear bomb went off at the Trinity Site in New Mexico, the radio played that very song.

The bomb, called the Gadget, was 1.5 meters in diameter. The Manhattan Project's funding totaled two billion dollars. The energy released by the fission of plutonium at its center generated heat reaching 66,000°C, eleven times that of the surface of the sun. Everything touched by its light burned.

Now Yōko is sixty-eight years old, and another of her daughters will become a mother.

After ten months and ten days, a baby will emerge from my belly.

And as it slowly opens its eyes, it will surely look into the light of the sun.

A TALE OF BURNING BOOKS

Passionate love is being expressed here by
a handful of wood, a bucket of coal,
a complete edition of books which lack humor and poetry.
Could you spare some Vladimir Illich Lenin?
Last winter has proven that his books burn well.

FAMA, *Sarajevo Survival Guide* (1993)

BELLFLOWER LAY WITH her head on Grandma's knee, looking out the window. Countless brand-new buildings glittered under the midday sun, reflecting the light like so many mirrors. It was the middle of summer, and the temperature outside was surely in the thirties; nonetheless, the air-conditioning made the room pleasantly cool. Grandma stroked Bellflower's long black hair for a while, then rustled around in the folds of her skirt, finally taking out a small can of Pocky.

"Don't tell your mother," she said.

Gleefully, Bellflower jumped up and took the can in both hands, opening it so she could carefully withdraw a single stick using her index finger and thumb. How wonderful, the shape of it! Like the twigs of the eucalyptus and acacia trees she'd seen on the internet. Bellflower ate the Pocky stick, making little crunching sounds. The sweet taste of cookie and chocolate filled her mouth.

"Of course I won't tell anyone, not Mama and not my friends either!"

More than keeping a secret from anyone in particular, Bellflower intended not to tell anyone at all. She had once told a friend at school about her weakness for Pocky, and in response, her friend had laughed meanly, asking in disbelief, "You really eat those things?" Bellflower knew this was her friend telling her that she couldn't believe anyone would willingly eat such gross old food. And it was true, Grandma bought her Pocky on the black market and kept it hidden in the back of the closet, so it was obvious it was the kind of thing people didn't eat anymore, that only old people cared about or wanted.

"After all, Grandma, chocolate's not good for you. Mama would get mad."

According to Mama, one should never eat anything too sweet or salty or oily—these were foods from the previous age, and people knew better now. Back when people ate such things, it was normal to die before you'd even reached a hundred, she said.

According to Grandma, though, Pocky was a thoroughly modern treat, and back when she was a little girl, her habitual luxuries were even more old-fashioned—black-bean senbei crackers, mochi-wrapped daifuku sweets, barbecued squid and tuna sashimi—strange-sounding foods that apparently everyone ate back then. Bellflower couldn't imagine what they might have been, but she could imagine Mama having a heart attack just hearing their names.

As she chewed on her Pocky, Bellflower wondered at the thought that there had been all sorts of people who ate such things, that Grandma had been one of them, that when she'd done so, she'd been around the same age Bellflower was now, back when Grandma hadn't been "Grandma" at all despite seeming like she'd been "Grandma" forever, Grandma since the old days before anyone could remember.

Back when Grandma was Bellflower's age, books had been made from trees. Their pages were paper, which came from forests like those she'd seen on the internet. You can see in the character for *book* (本) that books were the children of trees (木), that they shared the same roots. The character for *book* was also the character for *origin*, after all—books lay at the root of all things. This was how Grandma explained it.

These days, there were no more books, and no more trees, either—the acacia and eucalyptus Bellflower had seen on the internet, she'd never see in real life. All that was left were cities made of stone and metal and data. The tiny number of seeds left in the world—for cacao and millet, rice and wheat—only grew into fields of crops. None became trees that would grow into forests, then books.

In memory of all the plants that had been lost, parents took to naming their children after them. Soon children in their schools took the place of the forests and gardens of the past.

Bellflower had seen a book made of trees once in her life,

when she and her fellow botanically named classmates had gone on a school trip to a museum. The museum was made of brandnew stone that shone brilliantly in the sun, and inside they saw ancient "books" that were really tablets of stone and clay carved with characters that looked like pictures. But next to these, enclosed in a glass case and under heavy lock and key, there they were: two books made of trees, with pages made of paper. Their covers were shiny and vividly hued, one red, one green, and emblazoned across their fronts, the words: *Norwegian Wood*.

The museum guide spoke into her little microphone as she explicated the exhibit.

"Long ago, books were all made of paper like this, paper that came from trees. There were tens of millions of them, thousands of millions, all over the globe. We did not just lose trees and plants, books disappeared as well—books of all sorts, rare and valuable books, libraries full of books, all lost. This is a great tragedy. The two paper books that you see here were miraculously recovered in Japan, and we are lucky to see them."

Bellflower's classmate Sago Palm, who was standing next to her staring at the books as if trying to devour them with his eyes, whispered in Bellflower's ear.

"Do you know why these books survived?"

"Because they were very important to someone?"

At Bellflower's reply, Sago Palm smiled smugly at her and shook his head, pointing at the books in the case.

"It's because of the covers—that kind of slick, shiny paper is very hard to burn!"

Hearing this, Bellflower let out a little yelp.

"Sago! Have you ever seen a book burn?"

Sago Palm snorted and didn't respond. Nevertheless, this was the moment that marked Bellflower and Sago's transition from classmates into friends.

The two of them would spend all their time absorbed in conversation about paper books.

"Does this mean that way back then, there used to be woods in Norway?"

"It must!"

"If they had forests, that must mean they had lots of trees, and if they had lots of trees, they must have had lots of books!"

They could not stop talking about the books in the glass case, with their enticingly vivid covers.

"When I grow up, I want to work at that museum! That way, whenever I'm dusting the collection, I can reach in and take the books out myself, touch them, dust them, maybe even open them and see the paper myself!"

Sago seemed fascinated by Bellflower's fantasy and followed it up with one of his own.

"I'm going to become the richest man in the world, and then I'll buy that book so I can have it all to myself. I'll take it to bed with me and run my fingers over the words as I flip through the pages all I want."

"That would be amazing! How would it feel? What would it smell like? Oh, if you do get your hands on it someday, you have to let me touch it! Promise me. Promise me you'll let me or you'll swallow a thousand needles!"

"I'll swallow a thousand needles—a million! I promise."

Bellflower and Sago linked their pinkies together and sealed their pact.

But the books were destroyed only a month after they'd seen them and grown so enamored. In the middle of the night, an intruder broke into the museum, broke the glass case with a metal bat, and doused the books in kerosene before lighting them aflame. The white paper of the inner pages burned first, one after the other, ending with the difficult-to-burn shiny covers finally crumpling into bits of black ash that rose with the smoke into the air—this was the end for the last two-volume set of *Norwegian Wood* to exist in the world. Many theories were proposed for the motive: that it was the work of a terrorist, or someone mentally ill, or that it was a political crime. The news ran the footage of the book on fire over and over.

Bellflower watched intently as the footage of the burning book repeated, as if trying to devour it with her eyes. Grandma didn't approve.

When Grandma was young, a former president of a foreign nation had been executed by hanging and footage of the execution was shown, resulting in children imitating the footage and ending up hanging themselves. Bellflower heard Grandma's concerns and responded, "But there are no more books left in the world—how could I end up imitating it?"

"It's like Heine said," explained Grandma. "Where books are burned, in the end, people will also be burned.

"Though wouldn't it be nice if we never get to the point where we burn people again?" she added.

Bellflower didn't understand what Grandma meant by that, but she tried as hard as she could to imagine how a person might burn up and disappear into smoke the way the books had. But she could never really get her little head around it.

Yet, true to Grandma's word, the next thing to burn after the books was a person. Less than a month after the book burning, it was Grandma who died. She died, and was burned.

Bellflower was made to put on a nice blouse and a skirt in place of her usual jeans and found herself taken to a place called *the crematorium*. There was a crowd there, several families hearing the services of monks and priests, and after they gave their sermons and sutras to the various people assembled, all the families wept. Grandma was placed in the silvery, oven-like machine and burned up. Smoke escaped from the chimney above, but it was impossible to tell what smoke was Grandma and what might be any of the others burning that day. When Grandma came back out of the oven, she was just pale pink bones, and Bellflower and her mother used long metal chopsticks to transfer them one by one into a small box.

Bellflower clutched the long chopsticks and thought about how everything important to her—Grandma, the books—was burning up and disappearing, and she was filled with great sadness, tears running down her cheeks as she transferred the bones.

When she got home, she found the can of Pocky retrieved from Grandma's hiding place and carefully set on her bed—surely her mother's kindness. Bellflower fell asleep that night with the can held tightly in her arms.

. . . .

Sago came up to Bellflower, a downcast look on his face.

"It all burned up, huh?"

Bellflower couldn't tell if he meant Grandma or the books, so she just nodded silently in response.

She and Sago sat together on the seat beneath the window, and she took out the can of Pocky.

"Don't tell anyone."

Sago looked at the Pocky and didn't laugh or make fun of her. Instead, he asked, a sincere look on his face, "How do you eat something like that?"

Through the window, she could see countless brand-new buildings glittering under the midday sun, reflecting the light like so many mirrors, just like always.

"Like this."

Bellflower nibbled on one end of the stick, then pointed at the other end.

"Two people start eating at each end, and you meet in the middle."

"Like this?"

Sago put the other end of the Pocky in his mouth and began to nibble it. Soon they were nibbling the Pocky at both ends—a truly odd sight. The sweet taste of cookie and chocolate filled their mouths. Bellflower closed her eyes. She thought about the books that had burned up and disappeared. She thought of Grandma, who had burned up and disappeared as well. Bellflower and Sago's lips got closer and closer to each other.

This was the "Pocky Game." Grandma had taught it to Bellflower long ago, a twinkle in her eye. *You should try it when you get older*, she'd said with a smile. *Just don't tell your mother.*

Bellflower's lips touched Sago's. The Pocky stick had disappeared completely, so there was no more game to play, but they kept their lips pressed together anyway. Bellflower felt heat rising up within her, fire burning in the depths of her heart. There were books there, burning. And Grandma, burning too. Fire rose within her, flames licking up from her heart, warmer and brighter, and nothing would ever put it out.

PRECIOUS STONES

From darkness, I shall follow
A path into further darkness—
Shine on, O distant moon,
From the mountains' edge.

Izumi Shikibu (ca. 1000)

1.

Construction on the Ōedo Line had just begun. It was a deep hole they had to dig, and there were rumors that a hidden hot spring would be unearthed during the excavation—either that, or, since the site had once been used by the military, the white bones of the war dead.

But in the end, construction proceeded with neither water nor bones bursting forth, and the magenta-hued Ōedo subway line—then called Toei Line #12—opened in 1991. Later, a stop at Roppongi was added, which made it the deepest subway station in Tokyo.

The dark entrance during construction—I looked into its depths.

Way down there beneath the surface, so many distant places end up connected. Isn't that amazing?

I said this to someone; I was not alone.

Who had it been, standing there beside me?

She looks into the mirror. She's absorbed in the image, entranced, but not by herself—rather, she's staring at the jewel glittering upon her pale breast. Her name is Fumiyo. Her father owns the largest jewelry store in the Mikawa region of Aichi Prefecture. When she married into an X-ray technician's family in a neighboring town, she brought with her a paulownia hope chest filled to the brim with jewels (surely an exaggeration, but that's how she always described it).

Her hair is set into a permanent wave, its undulations setting off her lacquer-black, almond-shaped eyes. She's brushed white powder on the tip of her nose and rubbed a light rouge around her eyes and cheeks, following the "Makeup Techniques for Looking Beautiful beneath Streetlights" published in her beloved Housewife's Friend. *Beneath the electric light, her stomach swells conspicuously—her pregnancy is nearly to term.*

Her mother would say, for as long as she could remember, "Let me teach you the best way to tell a real from a fake."

Her mother is brushing her hair.

"Touch the diamond with a piece of radium. You'll be able to tell a real one from a fake right away."

Only a real diamond shines brilliantly at the radium's touch.

The year is 1929. The new Emperor's enthronement after the death of the Taisho Emperor took place just this past autumn.

Fumiyo turns slowly to look behind her. Her eyes meet mine directly.

And then I wake up.

I've had these dreams ever since the jewel came into my possession. These dreams starring a dead woman.

🔥

I opened my eyes and found myself in a minivan. The smell of the car heater filled the air, and soft rain fell beyond the foggy windows. Raindrops hit the glass, drawing lines before disappearing. I followed them with my eyes, thinking, *She was in my dreams again.* From the back seat, I looked into the rearview mirror. The jewel at my breast seemed to give off a faint light. I touched it with my finger and was about to close my eyes again, when my mother turned back toward me from the passenger seat and offered me some convenience store chocolate.

"Looks like I'm going to live a long time yet! I'm looking forward to the hot spring."

My mother was diagnosed with cancer almost immediately after my father died. Her death seemed so imminent that we'd even started discussing what to do with our nearly nonexistent inheritance, but then the radiation therapy worked and her cancer went into remission. To celebrate, we decided to go on a family trip for the first time in many years.

My eldest sister works at a travel agency and procured a stay at a hot spring resort for us. It was located near Ishikawa, in the southern part of Fukushima Prefecture, a place called Nekonaki Onsen—Cat's Cry Spring.

According to my sister, the spring's water is "resurrection water" and can cure any disease; it's a radium spring. The town is supposedly the birthplace of Izumi Shikibu as well, and nearby is the spring—the izumi—where she was first bathed after being born, as well as a rock said to be where she set her comb after using the water's surface as a mirror.

"It's perfect for Mom, and besides, it's the cheapest I could find."

It was a nearly all-female family trip with my mother, my three sisters, and me; the only male was my third-eldest sister's son. My sisters' husbands and boyfriends, out of either self-restraint or simple lack of interest, had all decided not to come.

My second-eldest sister ran a hand through her short, bobbed hair as her other hand gripped the steering wheel. Her job in sales at an apparel company involved a good deal of driving, and so she ended up taking over family chauffeur duties after our father died. As the rain intensified, she raised her voice in irritation as she made the windshield wipers beat faster.

"Aren't there a bunch of places that claim to be Izumi Shikibu's birthplace? I remember when I went to Saga, there was a

Zen temple that said she'd been born there. They even had a hanging scroll with some poems on it. And there were a bunch of supposed graves, too! Couldn't we have picked a place a little closer?"

We traveled north up the Tōhoku Expressway past Shirakawa, after which the traffic became steadily sparser as we continued northeast.

My third-eldest sister turned back toward her young son in the back seat and popped anti-nausea candy into his mouth, and then asked, with a line of worry creasing her brow, "A radium spring—isn't that radioactive? Are you sure it's safe?"

To which my eldest sister replied, touching a gel-manicured finger to her upswept hair, "If you don't like the place I found, you're free to stay somewhere else."

The boy in the back seat remained the only unconcerned party, silently absorbed in organizing his Yo-kai Watch trading cards. Our mother, sitting in the passenger seat with a map spread across her lap, found herself with time on her hands thanks to the GPS and began offering chocolate rather aggressively to everyone in the car.

"Too bad Dad's not still with us, he could have come too."

My second-eldest sister murmured under her breath in response.

"Dad never cared about a hot spring in his life."

Cat's Cry Spring was nestled in the crease between the mountains at the end of a narrow, winding road. Beyond the expanse of asphalt, trees showed the first faint signs of autumn color. Our bungalow, a two-story wooden building with a tile roof, was the most rustic of the various buildings, large and small, scattered around the area. The parking lot seemed vast in proportion to the number of buildings, and only a few cars dotted its surface. The rain still fell, but it had thinned to a near mist.

My third-eldest sister opened her eyes and cried out in relief as she pinned her hair back with a barrette. "Ah, finally—we made it!"

My second-eldest sister murmured under her breath again as she pulled the parking brake. "You can call it 'resurrection water' all you want, it's not like there'll be ghosts walking around or anything . . ."

My eldest sister grabbed her handbag and was the first to leap from the minivan, exclaiming, "What a nice place!"

A large noren cloth emblazoned with the resort's name hung in the entranceway. Beyond it, the interior was dim, but the floor was covered with vivid red wall-to-wall carpeting. We were shown to our bungalow after being handed traditional tea sweets. Several low seats typical of hot spring resorts were clustered in the center of the tatami room. My mother put her luggage down and immediately began boiling water in the electric kettle for tea.

"Wouldn't it be nice if a hot spring like this sprang up near my place?" she mused, addressing no one in particular.

◊

The house where my sisters and I were raised was located in the Nerima district of Tokyo, not far from Hikari-ga-oka—the Shining Hill.

Hikari-ga-oka used to have a military airstrip on it, and count-less planes flew south from there during World War II.

After the war's end, the US Army took over the area and built military family residences there, naming it Grant Heights after the Civil War general. My father moved there in 1973, the year Grant Heights was returned to Japan. Enfolded once more into Tokyo city planning, Hikari-ga-oka soon found itself filled with new housing, a waste processing center, and a large public park.

The construction of Hikari-ga-oka Park had begun the year before I was born as the youngest of four sisters, and by the time I started going to elementary school, both the park and the pure-white smokestacks of the waste processing center were fully op-erational. Soon after, tall, shiny apartment buildings sprang up all around us, and we couldn't stop staring up at them.

We stared because we'd heard that people jumped from them to their deaths. We'd heard that at night we might see ghosts.

My sisters and I were excited at the possibility of seeing a ghost or someone falling from the sky. Outside the Sunshine 60 build-ing in Ikebukuro (built not long before on the former site of the infamous Sugamo Prison), it was hard to think of another building tall enough to kill you if you jumped from it.

So, the four of us kept our eyes on the Hikari-ga-oka sky, waiting for someone to fall. But soon my sisters became preoccu-pied with shopping and dating, and the time we'd once spent staring up at the sky they spent more and more at IMA, the new shopping mall that had opened nearby.

IMA—the word glowed, spelled out in neon light.

I had learned my Roman alphabet, and I sounded the word out to myself again and again as I stared up at it.

I-M-A. IMA. Meaning *now*.

Abandoned by my sisters as they dated and shopped, I kept my vigil tirelessly, searching the skies between the tall buildings around me. Waiting for someone to fall.

⟁

The spring gushed forth from deep within the earth.

The mother bathed her child for the first time in its waters. It was the Heian Period, the year 978, the first year of the Tengen era. The spring's water turned a vivid red. The baby raised her voice into a loud cry. She was given the name Princess Tamayo.

Princess Tamayo grew up to be beautiful and clever, her black hair thick and lustrous and long. She always had her beloved cat clutched to her chest, and she could recite poems from the *Manyōshū* from a tender age. She looked into the water from the river's edge and used it as a mirror. Princess Tamayo washed her hair in the river and combed it with care, composing poems all the while. And then she set her comb upon a stone.

Word of her beauty and poetic prowess quickly reached the capital, and before long, Princess Tamayo had to leave home. She was just thirteen.

But her cat could not leave with her.

Overcome with grief, the cat cried for Princess Tamayo from morning till night. It eventually became so weak that it succumbed to illness and was near death.

But then, one day, the cat jumped into the spring, and its illness was miraculously cured.

And so the spring became known as Cat's Cry Spring, a name that has persisted even now, long after the cat and its mistress passed into the next world.

In the capital, Princess Tamayo was given a new name: Izumi Shikibu.

I read the pamphlet left on the table explaining the origin of the hot spring's name. To think, Izumi Shikibu was born at this very location exactly one thousand years before my own birth. A laminated map showing sites around the hot spring featured pictures of where she'd been bathed as a newborn, as well as the stone where she'd once set her comb.

I spread out all the pamphlets and maps I'd found in the folder and perused them.

A local historical museum pamphlet explained that the area was known for its veins of rare minerals; it featured photos of the aquamarines and crystals excavated there, as well as, more recently, radioactive ore. The cherry trees lining the banks of the river flowing past Ishikawa were apparently famous too.

Spreading out a tourist map of the greater area, I saw that part of the map was shaded gray—it had been declared off-limits after the Fukushima Daiichi nuclear disaster.

My mother picked up the pamphlet, her mouth stuffed with souvenir "hot spring" sweet-bean cakes, and began to read aloud the origin of the spring's name.

"So, if you take a dip in the spring, you'll live a longer life!"

"Why?" asked my sister's son from the floor, where he was laying his Yo-kai Watch cards out on the tatami.

My mother answered while pouring hot water from the electric kettle into a teapot. "There once was a cat who was very, very sick, and it jumped into the radium spring and got better. It's written right here."

"Cats don't swim—that's dogs!" he retorted, indignant. He fixed my mother with a grave look, and then added, "If a cat jumped in a hot spring, it would drown and die."

The "resurrection water" hot spring, where the cat supposedly took its miracle-cure dip, included an outdoor pool.

After eating a lavish dinner of typical hot spring resort cuisine—tempura and sashimi, nabe heated over a solid fuel burner, and so on—we began to visit the hot spring in shifts.

I went with my eldest and second-eldest sisters; we soaked together in the crystal-clear, odorless radium spring water. After a while, my sisters climbed out and walked unabashedly bare into the cold air outside, and we all headed toward the outdoor pool. Our chests looked like a diagram of Mendelian inheritance, my eldest sister's ample bosom contrasting with my other sister's and my modest endowments, the only feature in common being our small areolae.

The outdoor pool had a light illuminating it, but everything beyond the rocks and hedges at the pool's edge was engulfed in darkness.

My eldest sister stepped into the pool, wrapping a towel around her long, carefully upswept hair.

"It's been so long since we've all been together like this! Not since I got married, I think."

My second-eldest sister wrung out her towel and folded it neatly into a square to lay next to the pool before plunging into the water.

"When I think back to the four of us riding our bikes around Hikari-ga-oka, it feels like we've become a bunch of withered old maids. I wonder—if this water worked for that cat, maybe it'll work for us too and preserve us like this far into the future!"

I slipped into the water a little ways away from my sisters, my towel still wrapped around my body. I followed the white steam with my eyes as it wafted dreamily up from the water to be swallowed by the dark. Tipping my head back to look directly at the sky, I saw a full moon just barely beginning to wane.

My eldest sister seemed fully immersed now in the nostalgic mood with the others.

"Do you remember that urban legend we heard in Hikari-ga-oka? About the man who couldn't die?"

My other sister snorted scornfully from where she sat beside her.

"No—I don't remember that at all."

My eldest sister was fastidiously tucking stray hairs back into the towel around her head as she went on.

"I forgot what his name was, but people said there was a man who'd hang around IMA—he was immortal, and if you slept with him, it would cure you of any disease!"

"Wha-at?!" My second-eldest sister practically shouted, laughing. "Sleep with? You mean, have sex with?"

"Yeah, that's what I mean. You really don't remember?" murmured my eldest sister, absently stirring the surface of the water with her fingernails. "I can't believe you don't remember. There was that friend of a friend whose grandmother got cancer, she slept with him and then poof—the cancer went away! People talked about it . . ."

"Go, grandma!" my other sister said jokingly, then added, "We should have had Mom visit him, she could have bounced back faster."

I'd been quiet till then, but even I had to laugh at that.

But my eldest sister didn't crack a smile. "We should have. If it would have cured her cancer, we should have had her do it. I would, if it were me. I'd sleep with anyone."

My other sister laughed again as she began to massage her thighs.

"I'd never. Go to bed with some undead zombie man? Gross. You think he was just a pervert? Or was it some kind of scam?"

"Who knows?"

"I bet it was just a way to talk women into sleeping with him, simple as that." My second-eldest sister was scornful, but my eldest was still lost in her memories.

"I remember all the girls in my class talking about him. In the end, we decided to see what would happen if we all went together to go sleep with him. And we did—all us girls went together to Hikari-ga-oka to find him."

"What? You're joking!"

"But no matter how hard we looked, we could never find him. That's my spooky story."

The reflection of the light illuminating the radium spring undulated on the water's surface.

"The real horror was you girls, it sounds like!"

My second-eldest sister continued massaging her legs underwater.

My eldest sister stared out into the darkness beyond the light and said softly, "Maybe he was never really there at all. Maybe he was just the ghost of someone who'd jumped."

There was a brief silence, and then my sisters looked at each other. After a moment, they both burst out laughing.

I laughed along with them a little before silence fell once more.

I felt like I'd known the man they were talking about.

Who was it?

I couldn't quite remember.

My eldest sister's large breasts and my second-eldest's smaller ones floated in the hot water. I pulled my towel around me tighter and stirred up the water around me. Dark waves broke the light reflected on its surface into pieces.

My second-eldest sister asked, "When was this, anyway?"

My eldest sister thought for a moment, then answered, "I think someone said it was when the Showa Emperor died. The first year of Heisei. I remember on the way to Hikari-ga-oka talking with someone about how weird it was to say *Heisei* for the year instead of *Showa*."

My other sister crossed her legs underwater and sighed.

"The first year of Heisei—that was 1989, wasn't it? Nobody had cell phones then, or even beepers! I don't remember much from that time, really."

My eldest sister sank into the water as if about to slip beneath the surface entirely.

"We were pretty busy dating boys, I remember that."

Soon after, the three of us emerged from the pool, stretching our limbs, and that was the end of the conversation. In the changing room, my eldest sister spent an inordinate amount of time using a special brush under the hair dryer, while my other sister began stretching, still half-naked; I lay out in the tatami area, leaving my hair undried as I drank a Pocari Sweat.

The Showa Emperor died on January 7, 1989. I distinctly remember it. As His Majesty's condition worsened, laughter and music disappeared from the airwaves, replaced by grave-faced announcers reporting His blood pressure and the amount of blood discharging from His bowels—I took in more statistics and data about the decline of this person called the Showa Emperor than I ever did about the death of anyone I actually knew. Listening to the litany of numbers, I learned for the first time the real process of death—much more clearly and in greater detail than when my grandfather died, for instance.

The year began but no one wished anyone a happy New Year. Instead, a siren-like bell rang out one morning, and the television informed us over and over of the Emperor's death. It was a brand-new year, but the sky was dark and heavy with clouds.

By coincidence, an old woman living two doors down from us

passed away too, all alone, tucked into her futon. She had lamented her lot to anyone in the neighborhood who'd listen, wishing for an easy death so she could join her mother and father once again. Prayer beads in hand, she'd even started visiting those temples where elderly people pray for a quick and untroublesome death— prayers that, in the end, came true for her. But even when you die quietly in your bed, the police still come; flashing red lights illuminated her front door in the dark and silent night.

Yet no one spared her death a second thought. All the adults around me clutched their black umbrellas and hurried past her door to line up at centers the government had set up for citizens to register their condolences to the Imperial household. The television, too, persisted in broadcasting nothing but news about the Emperor's passing.

Japanese flags adorned with black ribbon began popping up here and there around the neighborhood. Looking at them as I walked past, I chose to imagine they were displayed in commemoration of the quiet passing of the woman from two doors down.

We emerged from the changing area and wandered around the dim hallways lit by the occasional fluorescent bulb, still in our yukata and with our hands full of wet towels and water bottles.

My second-eldest sister suddenly spoke up, as if she'd just remembered something.

"Hey, where's that stone Izumi Shikibu put her comb on, anyway?"

We picked up a black-and-white photocopied tourist map from the front desk and headed out to search for it. We figured it would be simple enough to find, but it proved elusive, and we searched around the resort in vain for a placard or anything to help us, the steam that clung to our bodies turning cold on our skin. Finally, we came across a small sign for it sitting between two larger ones pointing the way to his-and-her springs named for the god-and-goddess pair Izanagi and Izanami. The path indicated by the sign's arrow went up some stairs and then disappeared down some others, prompting my second-eldest sister to joke as we descended, "Welcome to the Land of the Dead!"

Eventually, we found ourselves in a small garden. There was indeed a large stone there, illuminated by a small light and fastidiously surrounded by a low fence.

My second-eldest sister snorted. "That's it?"

A small wooden sign nearby read THE FAMOUS STONE ON WHICH WAS PLACED THE COMB OF IZUMI SHIKIBU, followed by a brief recounting of the legend. But that was over a thousand years ago, and now, instead of a river running by to use as a mirror, there was a hot spring resort's foyer and banquet hall.

My eldest sister pulled out her phone.

"This is the Izumi Shikibu stone."

She took a picture. The phone's camera flashed.

"Mom, what are you doing? You shouldn't go in the hot spring with your rings on—the water will tarnish the metal and discolor the stones!"

My third-eldest sister was admonishing my mother as she got

ready to go to the hot spring without showing any indication that she planned to take off her jewelry. My mother, for her part, seemed not to even hear her and blew a white cloud of cigarette smoke out the open window by her side. And indeed, the fingers on the hand clutching the cigarette glittered with rings.

"It's so cold—can't you smoke outside? Or at least close the window? You really shouldn't be smoking in your condition, anyway . . ." My sister continued to complain, and my mother remained indifferent. The smoke she blew out the window disappeared into the dark as if inhaled by it.

"I'm sorry, but I have no intention of trying to work every one of these rings off just to go in the water. It would take forever."

She very deliberately took the portable ashtray from her pocket and stubbed her cigarette into it, then slid the window shut with a snap. She muttered under her breath, seemingly to herself, "Next, you'll be asking me to take my gold fillings out before I eat."

She likely couldn't slide her rings off even if she tried. She'd gained quite a bit of weight after our father died, and her rings bit deep into her flesh, seemingly on the verge of melding with it completely.

She jammed her feet into the brown slippers provided by the resort and strode into the hall, towel in hand, forcing my sister and her son to trail after her. The precious stones dripping from each hand shone with almost unnatural brightness in the hallway's dimly lit gloom.

Before he passed away, the only gifts my father gave my mother were jewels.

Our household was by no means wealthy, my father having given up his medical career to pursue one as a writer—indeed, you could say we were closer to poor. We knew no sushi beyond the kind that came on a conveyor belt; my sisters and I would fight over the strawberries on the Christmas cake. The expense of raising four daughters ruled out luxury in clothes or food.

Yet my father could never give up his jewelry, even if he had to go into debt to acquire it.

His mother's father had once owned the biggest jewelry store in Mikawa, after all. Making him the son of a jeweler's daughter.

His eyes would light up at the sight of a gem, whether in a department store or a museum, and even when he was dressed in threadbare, yellowed clothes, the fingers of both his hands would be covered in rings. Each set with its own precious stone.

Five years ago, in autumn, he passed away, and his body was placed in a cheap coffin, which in truth was not much of a shock—but his bare, ringless fingers were. Seeing them, I cried for the first time. Though his fingers had swelled so much no ring would have fit on them anyway.

After the funeral, the jewels from his mother—that is, our grandmother—were the only valuables left to divide between the four of us.

The one I received glowed, seeming to give off its own faint light.

And from the first evening I put it around my neck to lie against my breast, I've had dreams showing me her story. The story of my grandmother, Fumiyo. The story of a dead woman.

2.

The brightness of the sunlight reflected in the mirror from the window behind her makes her squint.

"It's annoying not to have the weather forecast. But no matter."

The trees in the garden outside the window are covered in deep green leaves. Is the sunlight so bright now because it's going to rain this afternoon? *she wonders to herself.*

The radio and newspapers stopped running weather forecasts after the attack on Pearl Harbor. The score from La dame blanche *plays on the radio, followed by the Japan Youth Symphony Orchestra playing "Silver and Gold," a waltz.*

She fans her chest slowly with a small fan. A drop of sweat slides down into the crease between her breasts.

No jewel lies against them.

She's given up her jewels for the sake of her country. Silver and gold, diamonds and amber and agates, rubies and sapphires—they call it household mining. Sumptuary laws forbidding extravagance have already forced her father's jewelry store to close its doors, despite it having once been the largest in Mikawa.

What will become of these precious stones? Will they be made into bombs? She has no idea. But she does not feel it as a hardship.

Though she can't help thinking back to Manchuria, where she'd gone shopping at the department stores in Harbin, the cobblestones glittering beneath her feet like jewels, streetlights and neon signs illuminating them as she passed by the art nouveau facade of Harbin Station;

she recalls the heavy overcoat she'd wrapped around herself to stave off the winter wind, cold and sharp enough to cut her ears, and she recalls the jewel that had glittered at her breast beneath that coat—and she can't deny the pang of nostalgia the memory brings.

Her husband had been assigned to work at the Japanese Imperial Army Hospital in Harbin, and they had gone to live there as a family—husband, wife, and young son.

"I wonder if it still feels like spring in Harbin?" she says softly, blinking, her eyes dazzled by the still unfamiliar Kanazawa summer sun.

The household moved back from Harbin when her husband got a new job at the Imperial Army Hospital in Kanazawa. This was but a brief stint for him, though, and soon he was back en route to Manchuria, part of the medical unit of the 13th Division of the Imperial Army as it crossed Shanghai's Garden Bridge into the Foreign Concessions.

She stares at me in the mirror. Her lips, gently touched with lipstick, slowly part.

"If otherwise the war would be lost and my husband and son killed, a few jewels are a small price to pay. I'll give them any they ask for."

I look at Fumiyo's chest; it looks even paler than before. As I do, my gaze meets hers.

And then I wake up.

I opened my eyes and found myself in a subway car. Eventually, I realized I was on the Ōedo Line—sitting at the terminus, in fact. Hikari-ga-oka Station.

Had I really drunk so much? When and where had I gotten on this train? And why? My memory was hazy. Wasn't I supposed to have changed, as usual, at East Shinjuku Station to the Fukutoshin Line heading for Narimasu on my way home from work?

I'd reached the middle of the platform when I put my hand to my mouth and ran to the restroom to throw up. After I'd exhausted myself vomiting, I stood before the dimly lit line of sinks and stared into the mirror.

I looked terrible. My eyes were puffy, with mascara clumped into dark shadows beneath them. I tried to use my hands to wash it off, but the sinks were broken—no water came from them. I had to make do with smoothing out my tangled hair with a comb.

As I did, the jewel at my breast gave off a faint glow.

I passed through the turnstile into the dense crowds passing to and fro as I headed for the exit closest to IMA. The voices of drunks belting out songs on their way home from end-of-year parties echoed throughout the underground passages, passersby swerving to avoid the pools of vomit lurking beneath the splash-marks on the tunnel walls.

I climbed the stairs on my way to the earth's surface and reached a landing. As soon as my feet touched it, I stopped, rooted to the spot.

I know this.

I tasted cold winter air.

I know this place.

I looked up to the surface from the landing.

There, from far beyond the lights in the windows of the apartment buildings of Hikari-ga-oka, the full moon shone back at me.

That's when I met him. I saw that man with my own eyes right here.

❧

I look into the depths of a deep, dark hole.

The Ōedo Line is still under construction. I am young, alone, making my way step-by-step down the stairs into the ground. I take a deep breath—it tastes of cold winter air and fine sand. The faint scritch-scratch of my sneakers' Velcro echoes off the tunnel walls.

I shouldn't go in. Of course I know I shouldn't. Nonetheless, I place first one foot onto a step, and then the other onto another, descending into the earth. My heart thuds in my chest. For what awaits me there, in the cavernous depths at the foot of the stairs, is surely the Land of the Dead.

After a while, even I grew tired of searching the Hikari-ga-oka sky for falling bodies, and my sisters and I turned our attention downward, absorbed by the depths of the hole being opened in the ground beneath us.

Construction had begun on the Ōedo subway line. We'd heard rumors that a spring or the bones of the dead might burst forth, feeding our excitement as we imagined the place deep beneath the earth where the Land of the Dead would be. We'd egg each other on, slipping past the tape cordoning off the construction site to see who'd climb the farthest down into the darkness.

"It's the Land of the Dead, so that means all the people who've ever died are down there, and all the animals too!"

"If you eat something while you're down there, worms get into your body!"

"If you look behind you as you climb out, you'll turn to stone!"

The four of us peered deep into the dark hole that had so suddenly appeared. But soon enough, my sisters tired of this too, shifting their attention back to shopping and dating, spending all their time in IMA instead of in contemplation of the earth's depths.

So I was left alone again to peer tirelessly into the darkness at the bottom of the hole. And, from time to time, I'd slip past the tape and see how many steps I could make myself take down into the depths.

The faintly shadowed stairs seemed to extend infinitely into the darkness beneath the earth.

On this particular day, I think I ended up descending farther than I ever had before, having glimpsed a faintly shining light in the darkness. The faint light drew me down toward it, and I felt exalted. I descended farther and farther down the stairs, guided by the light. My lungs chilled from within as the air around me grew colder. My breath would shine briefly white when I exhaled, drifting through the light before the dark swallowed it.

And so, there beneath the ground, in the dark depths of the Land of the Dead, I encountered not the people and animals who'd died before me, but rather the figure of a woman, naked from the waist down, clinging to a man.

. . .

The woman on the shadowy landing had her skirt hiked up and was moaning and screaming, tossing her hair wildly as she moved up and down. Thinking back now, she must have been in her late twenties or early thirties. But to me as a teenager, she seemed fully middle-aged. Her fleshy thighs hung in folds and the meat around her waist undulated like waves.

By contrast, the man she clung to struck me as oddly young, almost a boy. He wore a pure-white baseball cap, and his torso, wrapped in a too-big coat, was thin and delicate. The skin of his face and hands and the exposed lower half of his body seemed to shine, faintly illuminating the darkness around him.

One of the man's dainty, glowing fingers was being swallowed up into the woman's ass as he moved his hips back and forth.

The woman sucked his lips noisily. As she opened her mouth onto his, her breath became ragged as their tongues entwined.

The woman moved her hips, first slowly, then faster and faster. Liquid ran down her legs and dripped audibly onto the floor, and then, as if in concert, she began to cry out more and more intensely, as if the man were killing her.

Finally, she closed her eyes and took in a huge breath. Her entire body shuddered.

Aaaah!

The man closed his eyes as well and took a deep breath.

And then he slowly opened them.

The man's eyes met mine. They had no eyelashes around them. Their irises shone clear. I stood frozen, rooted to the spot.

Still staring straight at me, the man began to move his hips more vigorously. He worked his fingers between the woman's legs, deliberately spreading her open to show me her vagina.

Aaaah!

Stimulated by his fingers, the woman seemed to reach a point of no return, her body convulsing involuntarily.

My heart beat wildly—was she going to die here, right before my eyes? And was I going to be next? The man, his eyes still locked on mine, cried out in a sharp, loud voice.

Aaaah!

Trembling, the woman dug her fingernails into the man's flesh. White liquid began to trickle from her crotch.

But the woman hadn't died. She was breathing hard, her cheeks flushed red. Perhaps noticing the man's sightline, she slowly turned her head in my direction.

Our eyes met. I felt as if I were about to pee. The woman looked into my eyes.

"You should do this too, you know. Once you're older."

She drew her lips back, exposing her front teeth, and barked out a laugh.

"Every woman wants to stay young and beautiful, no matter how old she is. You're too young to know now, but you'll find out."

I walked past Hikari-ga-oka Park and headed toward Narimasu Station, turning my back to the moon. A red light blinked in the sky above the smoking area for the nighttime cleaning staff. When had I learned that the purpose of that light was to prevent airplanes from hitting the structure and falling to the earth? White breath swirled up from my mouth and disappeared into the dark.

I stopped at a convenience store on the way but ended up leaving without buying anything. The automatic doors opened and shut; cheery music played. After passing through the dark residential streets where streetlamps were few, I finally reached my apartment. Flipping the switch at the entrance, light shone through the glass window in the front door.

I dropped my down coat on the floor and collapsed onto the sofa. Empty beer cans and plastic convenience store bags littered the area around me. My cell phone began to ring. I picked it up and heard my third-eldest sister's voice.

I could hear her son reciting the names of the creatures from his Yo-kai Watch game in the background.

"The jewels!"

Jewels?

"I can't believe it—they're fake! The jewels are fake!"

Fake?

My third-eldest sister had apparently found out our grandmother's jewels, which we'd split between us after our father's death, were fakes. She'd brought them to an expert at the department store for an appraisal and the truth had come out.

"I don't know if only mine are fake, or all of them are—I just know we can't trust anything we got that isn't cold, hard cash!"

I peeled the stockings from my feet as I listened to my sister go on.

"I mean, it's not like I'd been planning on selling them right away or anything, it's just . . ."

I began to unbutton my blouse. I hadn't turned the heater on, and the cold air pressed in on my body as if to freeze it.

"It's just, I can't help thinking about money. Our son can go to a public primary school, but if he wants to go to private high school later, we'll have to pony up! And I felt Grandma would understand, since it was for her great-grandson, you know?"

I stood in the entrance of my bedroom in the dark, stripping off all my clothes without turning on the light. My skirt and blouse joined the tissues and magazines already littering the floor; they bloomed there like flowers. A woman's face smiled up from a magazine cover, her cheeks and the areas beneath her eyes radiant from skillfully applied makeup. My naked body stood reflected in the mirror leaning against the wall in front of me.

The jewel at my breast shone faintly, illuminating my body with its soft glow. I fell onto my futon and climbed between the frigid, stinking sheets. The cold cloth coiled around my exposed skin.

I heard my sister sigh on the other end of the phone.

"I really thought that stuff was valuable, you know? I'd put them in our safe! I feel like such a fool."

I closed my eyes.

Real? Fake?

Remember this, my child. How to tell the real from the fake.

Touch the diamond with radium and you'll know.

"In any case, it makes me feel so sorry for Grandma. A jeweler's daughter getting scammed with fakes! Ignorance is bliss, they say . . ."

My sister grew silent on the other end of the line for a bit, and then, as if unable to stand it anymore, she broke the silence with a laugh. "Well, I guess at this point, she's so blissed, she's the Buddha."

Her joking prompted a chuckle from me as well.

My sister's laughter continued for a bit, then abruptly stopped.

"Those jewels had always creeped me out anyway, you know."

My eyes opened wide.

Creeped you out how, sister?

Did you dream too?

Did you dream of the dead?

I was opening my mouth to ask, when my sister's son started crying and our call had to end.

I closed my eyes and tried to sleep.

I was still young as I stood there, looking up at the pale, overcast Hikari-ga-oka sky. I'd passed the age when I'd searched the sky for falling bodies, and I'd grown tired of peering deep into the ground as well, but I didn't really feel like joining my sisters at IMA either. It was March, but the air was still cold, my feet numb in their sneakers save for a tingling sensation at the tips of my toes. Only two months had passed since the Emperor's death, and it still felt strange to think this was all now Heisei.

"Waiting for someone to jump?"

I heard a man's voice behind me and turned to look at him.

It was him. The man whose cries I'd heard intermingled with the woman's in that underground stairwell. Now that I was seeing him in a well-lit space, his boyishness seemed all the eerier; while the taut skin peeking out from beneath his oversized coat no longer seemed to glow, it nonetheless stood out distinctly to my eyes.

Startled, I almost cried out.

He opened his mouth to speak, as if to soothe me.

"I've seen someone jump, you know."

I stared silently at him in response, then asked, nearly inaudibly, "Did they die? And you saw the body? Weren't you scared?"

Smiling as if drawing his skin even tauter, the man answered.

"I was jealous."

He paused, then went on.

"I was jealous because I can't die."

And then the man began to tell his tale in earnest.

The man told me he'd been born exactly one hundred years ago. The year he turned seven, a man in Europe named Röntgen caused a sensation by discovering rays he named X after the mathematical signifier of the unknown; the same year, a huge tsunami hit the northernmost part of Japan's main island.

The man grew up in a beautiful mansion and wanted for nothing, and his father treasured him dearly as his only son and heir.

But when he turned thirteen, disease struck and he ended up bedridden. His father poured his entire fortune into trying to save him, riding horseback across the country bearing as many jewels as he could carry, praying to every god and Buddha, and begging for help from every doctor, scientist, and snake-oil salesman who crossed his path. But his son only grew weaker.

Then one day, his father ran across a man selling medicine that glowed blue-white with what he called fairy light. If you take it, the man said, your body will become like this stone, and it will shine for more than sixteen hundred years without dimming.

At this point, the father had no servants left in his employ and had exhausted his fortune. The house itself had begun to collapse, and they sometimes lacked wood to stoke the fire to keep warm. Yet he didn't hesitate to hand over the last jewel he had left, a grand piece of quartz, to buy this medicine for his son.

A few days after his son began to take it, his hair fell out, first from his head and then from his whole body, and after a month, his skin began to flake and peel off as well, with new, taut skin appearing beneath. This new skin seemed to glow, as if lit from within.

And thus the son attained his form, finding himself in a body that wouldn't die. He decided then to call himself Quartz.

But I was no longer a silly child willing to believe such a ridiculous story. Or at least that's what I told myself, childishly.

And so my reply was a bit cruel.

"So you can't die, huh? Prove it."

Word of the man who could not die eventually reached the capital. They said that sex with him would cure any sickness—typhus, the plague, even cancer. Hearing this, women from all over came to him, opened their legs, and mounted him. A marketplace with souvenir stands sprang up around his house, and elsewhere other competing counterfeit immortals appeared as well. These pretenders promised not just to cure illness but to preserve youth and beauty, too—*One touch and you'll glow as if bathed in moonlight*, as one slogan put it.

But then the war began, and the man found himself arrested again and again. Each time, though, the women seeking to prolong their lives came to his rescue, bailing him out of prison and continuing to make love to him in secret. Even after the war ended, he remained in hiding, passing his days in shadow. But women never stopped coming to him, begging him to cure their illnesses, to preserve their youth and beauty. He met them in that stairwell deep within the earth and satisfied their desires.

The man called Quartz pointed up at the Hikari-ga-oka sky.

"You want me to fall from up there in front of you to prove I can't die?"

I looked up, following his finger with my eyes. Quartz lowered his hand and stroked my cheek. He brought his face toward mine as if to eclipse it, then kissed me.

"I just added a year to your life," he said as our lips parted slowly, our commingled breath rising white from between us to touch the cold sky.

I looked into Quartz's eyes. He had no eyelashes, just as I remembered, and his irises were clear.

"You're a liar."

Those clear eyes, that taut, glowing skin—he was so beautiful.

"And besides, another year means nothing."

What's another year, anyway? What good does that do me?

I wanted to live a lot longer than that. I wanted never to die, like him.

After all, if I died now, I'd be gone and forgotten in an instant.

When school started again, I went to the library and checked out a reference book on minerals. I hadn't believed Quartz's fairy tale in the slightest, but I nonetheless flipped to the entry on quartz.

The photo showed a piece of quartz against a jet-black background; it was beautiful. I learned that clear stones like these were called crystals. The smooth, translucent sides of the hexagonal crystal in the book reminded me of Quartz's taut skin.

Crystal. Quartz.

When quartz crystals come in contact with alternating current, a resonance occurs. They resonate at precise frequencies, these crystals. Around a hundred years ago, Pierre Curie's discovery of this property led to crystals being placed in clocks; crystals keep time for us even now.

Why was it that in my heart of hearts, I longed to believe in this man, to believe in Quartz? That his existence and everything else he'd told me wasn't a lie, that he would never die, that he'd lived a hundred years and would live a thousand more?

Was it because I wanted him to remember me, even far into the future?

How to tell the real from the fake.

But real or fake, neither of us would be around a thousand years from now, would we? Our lives would be the stuff of rumor at best.

I curl slowly into the sheets on my bed. I close my eyes. Awaiting dreams. Dreams of the dead. Dreams of her.

3.

Her long, thin fingers touch the light reflected on the surface of the water, breaking it into pieces.

With the worsening of the war, there are fewer and fewer chances to take a proper bath like this, and she knows how lucky she is to afford such luxury. She'd had to wait so long in line, and it's so crowded that the tub's lid has been lifted again and again, the water losing heat and growing tepid, but the fact remains that it simply feels good to shed her clothes and submerge herself in water. Still, she can't help but sigh. It's true that it's all starting to get to her—washing her face with strange-smelling laundry soap instead of the imported kind that comes in a red box, sewing five- and ten-sen coins into an endless stream of sennin-bari good-fortune belts to send to soldiers on the front lines. But that's not the only reason she sighs.

Shortly after moving to Kanazawa, her only son took ill. X-rays were taken and medicine prescribed, but he grew worse by the day. By the time the doctor warned that he was nearing death, her mother, who'd traveled a great distance to help her daughter, told her about a spring whose waters were said to cure any disease. There may have been no more treasures left in the jewelry store in Mikawa, but her mother remained as forceful as always.

"Back when the Taisho Emperor was still alive, there was a special train that took people to the spring—it's a radium spring, you know. Everyone wanted to take a dip in it. They said it would cure anything. Typhus, plague, even cancer. You could buy radium rice crackers as souvenirs. The radium makes your skin young again, makes it shine."

She watched her mother as she spoke, distracted by the glints of gold deep within her mouth. The thing was, if such a spring really existed, no one would ever die. There was no reason to believe such a superstitious tale. But she remembered an article she'd read in the newspaper a while ago, in the special edition for the 2600th Anniversary of the

Founding of Japan. It told of an experiment conducted for the public at the Tokyo Military Hall in which a famous scientist created what he called a radioactive man. The man had been given man-made radium to swallow, if she recalled correctly. And so, thinking of this, she sold her very last jewel, which she'd kept hidden from authorities, on the black market and bought a ticket for herself and her son to go to the radium spring.

And then what happened? She took him to the spring, and within a month, somehow, his illness was cured.

What value can any jewel have compared to his life? I'd give up any number of them to keep him with me.

She repeated this to herself again and again. Yet that had been her last—after that, she had no more left to give.

She remembers the indescribable joy with which she'd watched her son rise from his sickbed.

After his miraculous recovery, her son applied himself diligently to his studies, and he ended up passing the entrance exam to the prestigious Fourth School. She swelled with pride imagining him walking through the Kanazawa streets wearing the school's black coat, the four-pointed North Star on his cap dazzling all who saw it.

But before he'd had a chance to don the cap even once, he was called away for student mobilization. He was assigned to the Inami airplane factory in Toyama Prefecture. Her son packed his things happily, even writing patriotic slogans on spare newspaper like Brave Students, Join the Special Kamikaze Forces—To the Front Lines!

On top of this, her husband, despite finally returning to Kanazawa, was now deployed onboard the Heian Maru, *shuttling back and forth to Rabaul on the island of New Britain in Papua New Guinea, a jour-*

ney perilous enough that he'd left behind his last will and testament just in case.

If I'd known it was going to end up like this, perhaps I wouldn't have exchanged my last jewel for a trip to some pool of magic water.

After all, no one knew when the next airplane factory would be bombed. She should have grown accustomed to the constant air-raid warnings, yet she still startled every time the siren blared. Wouldn't it have been better to die at home, in bed, than on some factory floor?

When would Japan build its own great bomb, anyway? A bomb small as a matchbox but powerful enough to bathe New York or London in flames. Come to think of it, she'd heard rumors that a famous scientist—a graduate of the Kanazawa Fourth School, in fact!—was hard at work creating such a weapon. She longed for him to return to his hometown, wreathed in glory at its completion.

This dream weapon was meant to drop on Saipan. If Japan could take Saipan back from the Americans, they'd no longer have a place to refuel on their way to bomb the mainland, and the constant air raids would finally stop. She'd live free from the fear of bombing once more. Free from the fear of death.

Her body floats in the water; her ample breasts bob to the surface. She sees their small nipples and her breath catches in her throat. She remembers reading in her Housewife's Friend *an article that purported to tell readers' fortunes based on the shape and size of their breasts. "The children of women with small nipples were in danger of misfortune," it said.*

What a disaster everything has become.

She slowly emerges from the water. Her heat-flushed body is unadorned, but water drips from her breasts like jewels.

Slowly, she turns her head toward me. Her line of sight meets mine.

And then I wake up.

I opened my eyes and found myself in a room with gray industrial carpeting. The walls were covered in posters advertising free new cell phones if customers act now. I was sitting in front of a computer, a rainbow-colored screen saver bouncing around its monitor. A cell phone was sitting on the table in front of it, vibrating. I stared at it, thinking about how even newfangled phones like these had crystals deep within them. When I picked it up, I heard my eldest sister's voice on the other end.

"What are we going to do if Mom dies?"

I could hear station announcements and train sounds in the background.

"I saw Mom in Ikebukuro the other day, and she seemed off to me, you know? She told me she'd been having crazy dreams. I'm getting worried about her."

I kept my eyes on the rainbow screensaver bouncing in front of me.

My sister's voice droned on, occasionally swallowed by the background din.

"I've been thinking about Grandma lately."

"Grandma?"

"You know, Dad's mom. Grandma Fumiyo. With the jewelry? You're too young to have met her, but I remember her."

According to my sister, Grandma Fumiyo, just before she died, had suddenly started talking about having strange dreams. Concerned, our father had rushed all the way to Tokyo to visit her, but it was already too late—by the time the cancer was discovered, it had progressed so far that there was nothing to be done about it.

"She talked about seeing her 'fourth grandchild' in her dreams. It creeped me out!"

Her fourth grandchild? In other words, me?

I was about to ask about this, but my sister continued talking without giving me a chance to break in.

"Well, I mean, dreams or no, the question is: What are we going to do if Mom's cancer comes back? I haven't been able to stop thinking about it all day."

Having finally said it all out loud in one go, my sister finished the call by adding, apologetically, "I mean, just—what if? What if? That's all, you know."

The little song signaling a train departure played in the background.

I was still sitting there, staring blankly at my computer, when two girls clutching makeup cases passed by my desk. One of them wore sparkling lamé mascara, and she stopped short and turned in my direction, whispering to her friend, "Hey, over there—what do you think? Real or fake?"

The rainbow screen saver on my monitor suddenly disappeared, revealing the desktop. I froze where I sat, unable to move. But then I noticed that the girl was looking past me at a man across the room.

The man had quite unnaturally dark hair. The other girl snorted.

"So fake. Fake as your tits."

♦

My second-eldest sister was driving the four of us down the streets where we used to ride our bicycles together so long ago. At our eldest sister's urging, we'd decided to go together to check up on Mom in person.

Commentators on the radio were talking about how it was the fifth anniversary of the Great East Japan Earthquake. And indeed, now that they mentioned it, the day before yesterday had also been the anniversary of the carpet-bombing of Tokyo.

The white towers of the Hikari-ga-oka waste processing plant rose into the sky before us. A song started playing on the radio.

"This is 'Welcome to New York,' by Taylor Swift, from her album *1989*."

1989, the year Taylor Swift was born. The year the Showa Emperor died. The year I met Quartz.

Already twenty-seven years ago.

My third-eldest sister was fiddling with her barrettes as she said, "Still, I was disappointed about Grandma's jewels."

My second-eldest sister, her hands on the wheel, snorted her agreement.

"You don't have to tell me—I'd kept them locked up in a safe until just now."

My eldest sister turned back from the passenger seat.

"I don't think we should have the rest of them assessed. As long as there's a possibility they're real, we can dream they are."

My third-eldest sister cut in, raising her voice a little.

"If that's what you think, why don't you wear them?"

"You know I can't! I'm allergic to metal!"

My second-eldest sister snorted softly.

"I can't wear them due to company policy. We handle accessories of our own, after all."

My third-eldest sister made a face as she chewed on her anti-nausea candy, but said nothing.

The car continued its way down the road. Through the windows, we could see the bare-limbed trees lining the street sliding past, interrupted by the park's wide expanses of still-brown grass. The sign for IMA rose on the park's far side, and my second-eldest sister, catching sight of it, said, "Oh, I meant to say—I remembered something. About what we talked about at the hot spring."

She said she remembered now that there had been a pervert who'd show up from time to time around IMA. The school had even distributed flyers warning students about him. The description of the pervert in the flyers seemed to match the description of the man who couldn't die, she said. Maybe it was the same guy!

"He used the same line, you know. 'Sleep with me and I'll

cure you, sleep with me and you'll be young and beautiful.' Really perverted stuff like that."

My eldest sister's eyes lit up as she heard this. "Just like I said! So it's not just me!"

"But I mean, how could people be pulled in by that? It's like a joke! 'You want to feel better? Sleep with me! Want to be young and beautiful again? Sleep with me!' What were people thinking?"

My eldest sister's voice was heavy with irony as she responded.

"I remember you buying all those weird supplements when Mom got sick . . ."

My second-eldest sister exploded. "That's not the same thing at all! Those supplements work! They might have been what cured her, you don't know!"

My third-eldest sister had kept her silence during this exchange, but now she pulled her seat belt to loosen it and leaned forward.

"I don't remember as much about it, but I can't help but wonder—could you really sleep with a guy and wake up young and beautiful again?"

The car crossed Sasame Boulevard. The black earth of daikon fields started to appear on both sides of the road. But in many places, there were newly constructed housing developments where fields had been. The car came slowly to a stop at a light, right in front of a convenience store that also seemed to have just been built.

My second-eldest sister, her hands still firmly clutching the wheel, looked into the rearview mirror at the seat behind her.

"So what would you do if it *were* true? Would you sleep with him?"

❀

The little house where we spent our youth was still the rather run-down structure we all remembered, seeming, as always, on the verge of tipping over completely. A white cat raced out as soon as we opened the door. The inside of the house smelled faintly of mold and was so drafty it chilled us as we entered. The foyer, though, which had always been so cluttered, was now eerily tidy; we exchanged puzzled glances at the sight.

My second-eldest sister murmured, "This is a bad sign . . ."

My eldest sister seemed to agree, saying in a low voice, "It looks like Mom started final prep, doesn't it?"

My third-eldest sister slid her feet into a pair of the slippers that had been so neatly lined up in front of the step up into the house proper. "Final prep?" she asked.

My second-eldest sister looked faintly irritated as she answered. "You haven't heard of that? You know how there's a set of things you do as you plan a wedding, right? Well, there's this trend now where people do the same thing planning their own deaths—buy a grave marker, write their will, clean out their place . . ."

The white cat lingered at the door with us, seeming to listen to our conversation as it wound itself around our legs and wriggled its hips to get our attention.

Just then, Mom opened the door to the kitchen, emerging

from its depths. The hot smell of the gas heater wafted through the door with her.

She seemed well, not withered or gaunt at all. If anything, she seemed more full-bodied than usual; in any case, she hardly seemed to be in the late stages of cancer, and was full of good cheer as well.

"I bought cake for us!"

There was a small Buddhist shrine set in the corner of the kitchen, and we took turns clasping our hands before it. Photos of various relatives decorated the shrine; our father's black-and-white portrait sat right in the center in its black plastic frame. Next to him was his mother, Fumiyo. She had died much younger than our father had, and so, at least in their black-and-white portraits, they looked like brother and sister.

Perhaps that's how it'll be for all of us, eventually—all our distinct roles as grandmothers or mothers or fathers or daughters lost to time, everyone just a series of siblings in photos. My older sisters rang the little golden bell and lit the incense.

"That's not a good sign . . ."

My second-eldest sister said this to me under her breath, indicating the white chrysanthemum placed carefully next to the bell along with fresh offerings of rice and tea. We'd never seen our mother so pious. Thin ribbons of white smoke rose from the glowing red ends of the incense sticks.

The cake Mom bought was a strawberry shortcake already cut into portions, not a whole cake like the ones she used to bring home at Christmas, so there was no need for us to fight over the strawberries. She made instant coffee and served it to us in one too many mugs, then sat down at the place farthest from the door and dug zestily into her piece.

"There's something I wanted to talk to you kids about . . ."

Here it comes—we braced ourselves for what she was about to say. But Mom stopped speaking, her fingers still gripping her fork, and silence descended upon the table. White steam wafted up from the mugs in front of us.

Finally, unable to stand it any longer, my eldest sister spoke.

"Mom, you don't need to hide—you can tell us anything!"

My second-eldest sister pressed further.

"It's true, Mom. What would we do if you just disappeared one day without telling us anything?"

Shocked, Mom jerked her hand. Whipped cream flew from her forkful of cake onto the floor.

"It's not—I'm not—"

The white cat darted over and began licking the spilled cream.

"I'm not *dying*. I met someone!"

A man who had worked as a caregiver for our father had apparently kept dropping by even after his death, helping with shopping or tidying up. It became clear after a while that this man had feelings for Mom, and Mom didn't mind him either, now that she thought about it—this is how she explained it to us.

Mom blushed.

"He's a bit younger than me, though . . ."

She continued, more abashedly than before.

"He got me started on hula lessons. His younger sister lives— oh, what is it called now? It used to be the Jōban Hawaiian Center, now it's, that's right, it's called Spa Resort Hawaiians. She grew up near there and danced hula since she was young, he said. So of course her dancing's a whole different kettle of fish than mine, having done it all her life . . ."

Then Mom added, as if it had just occurred to her, "Remember last year when we went to that hot spring? It turns out that his father's from there! From Ishikawa, where we went! Maybe we were called there."

My sisters and I exchanged a glance.

"Called there? By whom?" My second-oldest sister murmured this half to herself, but Mom didn't answer. And besides, however strange, this was much better news than that her cancer had come back.

It turned out this man was a considerate gentleman, bringing fresh flowers for the shrine when he visited, lighting the incense, and replenishing the rice and tea offerings. So there they were, explanations for all the ominous signs we'd observed. By the time everything was cleared up, the instant coffee in the extra mug had cooled completely. My eldest sister brought it up.

"Mom, you set out an extra cup of coffee, you know."

Mom rose from her seat without answering and walked over to stand beneath the air vent, putting a cigarette in her mouth and lighting it with a plastic lighter. As always, her fingers glittered with jeweled rings that seemed so embedded in her flesh that they'd never be slid off again.

White smoke curled languorously up from our mother's mouth.

"Your father was a wonderful man. But I'm still alive, and I plan to continue to be for a long time yet."

The jewel at her breast seemed to glow with faint light.

My childhood bedroom was located right at the top of the stairs. It, at least, remained essentially unchanged, the furniture draped in white sheets. My three sisters had all left, but I'd decided to stay the night there. A sofa bed sat in the corner of the room, and I pulled it out to sleep on. I stared up at the knotted wood grain on the ceiling, another thing that had remained unchanged since I'd been young. I traced its curves with my eyes, letting them lead me back into the past.

"It's the Land of the Dead, so that means all the people who've ever died are down there, and all the animals too!"

"If you eat something while you're there, worms get into your body!"

"If you look behind you as you climb out, you'll turn to stone!

My sisters were always saying things like this to me.

I was young, alone, making my way step-by-step down the stairs into the ground at the construction site, a jewel gripped in my hand.

I'd decided that if the only other option was dying, I'd rather turn to stone.

It was a sincere decision.

No matter what sort of place turned out to be down there—the Land of the Dead or wherever—I'd made up my mind: I was going to look behind me on my way out.

Quartz was on the landing, waiting for me. As always, his taut, pale skin glowed softly in the dimness.

"I'll make it so when you die, you'll turn to stone."

I placed the jewel I was holding onto Quartz's palm just as I'd promised. It was my birthstone, given to me by my father.

Quartz enclosed the jewel in his shining, slender hand.

"Stone never dies, and never forgets. It remembers everything that happens to it—every little thing, down to the smallest detail—and preserves it all inside itself."

I looked deep into Quartz's eyes. His lashless eyes, with their clear irises—they were so beautiful.

"Even after a hundred years? A thousand?"

"Even after a million."

"So that means, let's say, if I were to become a stone myself, then that stone would remember me forever too, right?"

I remembered the grand procession of black cars I'd seen on TV. They'd rolled slowly along in the rain. Politicians and celebrities from around the world had gathered to take part in the ceremony. I counted the cars as they passed and imagined that this grand ceremony was in honor of the old woman who'd lived down the street.

"Even if I never become great?"

"Even if you never become great."

His words soothed me to my core.

He didn't tell me that everyone was great, or that everyone was important—Quartz didn't deal in empty platitudes. I took great solace in that.

I'm fine just as I am. I don't have to become great, I don't have to become my "true self," or anyone else for that matter, I can just be like this and it won't be all for nothing. Even an existence like mine can be remembered.

"Swear to me. Pinky swear! Swear that if you break this promise you'll swallow a thousand needles."

I hooked my pinky finger to Quartz's. His finger was slender and a little rough, but glowed faintly—I wanted my finger to be hooked to his forever.

"Pinky swear!"

Our fingers slowly unhooked from each other.

"Even if you swallowed a thousand needles, you wouldn't die, so I guess this is all pretty meaningless for you."

I told this little joke and burst out laughing. Quartz's luminous skin stretched even tauter as he laughed too. And then his lips met mine, again and again. My body became illuminated with his light. I let my lips, my tongue, meld with his, just as I had seen that woman do.

But where had it gone, the jewel my father had given me?

My eyes were closed but I couldn't sleep. I finally rose from the sofa bed and walked down the stairs. The jewel at my breast began to vibrate slightly as I did. I turned on the gas heater. The white cat appeared from nowhere at my feet, churring softly. I sat down before the little shrine and pulled a few books from the nearby shelf to look at.

One of the books was a history of Ishikawa and the area around Cat's Cry Spring. Did Mom's considerate new gentleman caller give it to her, or had she bought it herself during our trip? Whatever the case, as I leafed through the pages, I encountered headings like "Ishikawa's Rare Ore," "The Ni-Go Project," "This Rare Element," and so on.

It seemed that Ishikawa's soil yielded rare minerals, including

63

radioactive ore. I recalled that the springs there were radium springs, and that I'd seen pamphlets from the local historical museum introducing the different kinds of ore.

But what was "The Ni-Go Project"?

It turned out that this was the name for the top-secret program carried out under the auspices of the famous physicist Yoshio Nishina to develop a "uranium bomb"—that is, a nuclear bomb—during World War II.

In 1941, at the request of the Japanese Imperial Army, a top-secret project was undertaken to build a nuclear bomb for Japan.

Approximately ten kilograms of Uranium-235 were needed to make such a bomb.

The search for Uranium-235 thus began. From the Korean peninsula to Malaysia, as soon as a territory was invaded, the earth was turned over and stones extracted to be tested.

But ten kilograms of Uranium-235 remained elusive.

An attempt was made to bring the uranium from Europe in a Nazi U-boat that crept along the Atlantic Ocean floor, but in the end this strategy failed too.

Meanwhile, the search for domestic sources of uranium continued. The man heading up the search, from excavation to refining, was a graduate of Kanazawa Fourth School, the physicist Satoyasu Iimori. Dr. Iimori had been gathering and studying the ore from the Ishikawa area for a long time, and now a white-feathered arrow had been placed on the map where radioactive ore slept beneath the earth.

Air raids continued in Tokyo even after the carpet-bombing, and the research center was relocated to Ishikawa. Mobilized students gathered there, clearing runways to make airfields on the one hand and digging deep into the ground with dynamite and earth-moving nets on the other.

Mom woke up while I was still reading. Muttering to herself that I'd left the gas heater going, she looked over and caught sight of the book in my hand.

"Ironic, isn't it? Before we had a chance to finish making our own nuclear bomb, two got dropped on us."

She walked over to stand beneath the air vent and light up a cigarette.

"Or maybe we succeeded by failing to make one, in the end."

Let me teach you the best way to tell a real from a fake . . .

I turned to Mom. "What's the best way to tell a success from a failure?" I asked.

White cigarette smoke floated languorously upward only to disappear, swallowed by the air vent.

The white cat cried out loudly from where it sat at my feet.

Mom took the book from me and leafed quickly through it with her jewel-encrusted fingers. She stopped at a page with an array of photos on it.

"I've been seeing these in my dreams lately."

The photos showed jewels of various colors.

Dreams of who? Of the dead?

Of my father?

I was on the verge of asking her when I drew up short.

The jewels in the photos looked like the ones we'd inherited from Grandma Fumiyo.

Next to them, there was text.

After the end of World War II, the Occupation government naturally forbade not only the development of nuclear weapons technology, but all research related to radioactivity. This of course meant that Dr. Iimori could not continue his work excavating and refining uranium ore under the auspices of the Ni-Go Project.

Due to this, Dr. Iimori, while remaining in Ishikawa, ended up turning his attention to the use of radioactive ore to create gemstones.

After years of research, Dr. Iimori had produced a rainbow of precious man-made stones: Victoria Stone, Gamma Zirconia, Sun Diamond, Synthetic Quartz Eye, and so on.

In short, while his dream of creating nuclear weapons never came true, in their place he created precious stones, radiant with light.

Ash fell from the end of the cigarette in Mom's mouth.

"Can a jewel retain the memory of someone's life, I wonder? So if you wear it, you'll see that life in your dreams?"

4.

She looks into the mirror. A grand jewel glitters upon her breast, just as before, but instead of being entranced, she's brought up short.

The war had ended. The government had mobilized her son to work at an airplane factory, but he had escaped death—before an air raid could strike the factory, two nuclear bombs had been dropped, one on Hiroshima, the other on Nagasaki, and Japan had surrendered.

But she had no reason to know that that rumored bomb of her dreams, that bomb meant for Saipan that wasn't completed on time— she had no reason to know it was the same kind of bomb as the ones dropped on Japan.

The Emperor's voice was broadcast over the airwaves. She heard that voice, the voice of the Showa Emperor, the voice of a man who was also a god. The broadcast kept cutting out, though, so it was difficult to grasp what that voice was actually trying to say.

Her husband had lost his vocation as a military doctor, and he was forbidden from public service by the Occupation government; her family's jewelry business had been destroyed during the war; MacArthur's GHQ had transformed the Emperor from god into human; but she herself remained as she had always been: a jeweler's daughter. Even as her hands were bare of even a single jewel.

No matter how hungry she got, more than dumpling soup, more than chocolate, what she desired most were jewels.

She wanted it all back—her jewels, her past—she wanted every little thing she'd lost returned to her, back to the way it had been.

Quite a bit of time passed following the war's end before precious stones came into her hands once more. No one knew where she'd found them— what department store or jeweler—or how much she'd had to pay, but what was certain was that one day a grand jewel lay upon her breast again just as it had before. The only difference was that, rather than glittering with reflected light, this new jewel seemed to glow softly from within.

But by the time this new, glowing jewel appeared at her breast, her son had long since left home and gotten married, and in fact had already had three children, and her cancer was in its latter stages. Her husband had regained his medical practice as a village doctor again, but it seemed as though he hadn't been able to see the sickness of his own wife.

She's so thin, standing there before the mirror. Slowly, she turns her head to look behind her.

Her eyes meet mine directly.

🜂

I opened my eyes and found myself in a train station. But not an Ōedo Line subway station. This unknown station was made out of wood and seemed brand-new. There was a sign written in old-fashioned characters: Aichi Electric Railway Company. A train made up of matchbox-style cars lit up with electric bulbs slid into the platform. Men and women dressed in kimonos stepped out of the train, umbrellas in hand. A newspaper tucked beneath one of their arms showed the year to be in the Taisho period. The train began to move again, sliding back out of the station.

Under my breath, I murmured something to myself.

Way down here beneath the surface, so many distant places end up connected. Isn't that amazing?

The next thing I saw was Quartz. He looked boyish as always, and his skin glowed softly in the dimness. But instead of a too-big coat, he wore a too-big kasuri-patterned kimono.

Quartz was waiting for someone.

A girl emerged from the darkness, dressed in Western clothes and with a large jewel resting upon her breast. I realized I knew her. She was Grandma Fumiyo as a young woman. On her feet, she wore black leather Mary Janes.

"I'll make it so when you grow old and die, you'll turn to stone."

Just as she'd promised, she gave Quartz the jewel she held in her hand. It was her birthstone, given to her by her father.

Quartz enclosed the jewel in his shining, slender hand.

"Stone never dies, and never forgets. It remembers everything that happens to it—every little thing, down to the smallest detail—and preserves it all inside itself."

She looked into Quartz's eyes. They were lashless, the irises clear.

"Even after a hundred years? A thousand?"

"Even after a million."

"So that means, let's say, if I were to become a stone myself, then that stone would remember me forever too, right?"

She thought about the commemorative picture-postcard book in her house—the Crown Princess in her one-piece dress and flower-covered hat, the Crown Prince in his Mandarin-collared uniform, his breast covered in medals, soon to become the Showa Emperor. They were photographs taken during their wedding, which had only recently taken place, having been delayed due to the Great Kantō Earthquake. Everywhere was still wrapped in an atmosphere of celebration. Tokyo, the Imperial Capital, was on the road to reconstruction. But beneath the glorious capital she imagined, deep down at the bottom of its wells, the corpses of those massacred in the earthquake's aftermath still lay where they'd been thrown, never to be discovered.

"Even if I never become great?"

"Even if you never become great."

Quartz nodded deeply.

"Even if I never become important?"

"Even if you never become important."

As she listened to his reassurances, her face lit up.

"Swear to me. Pinky swear! Swear that if you break this promise you'll swallow a thousand needles."

She hooked her pinky finger to Quartz's.

"Pinky swear!"

Their fingers slowly unhooked from each other.

"Even if you swallowed a thousand needles, you wouldn't die, so I guess this is all pretty meaningless for you, isn't it?"

Slowly, she turns her head to look behind her. Her eyes meet mine directly.

◊

She handed her jewels to her son, who had rushed to her side all the way from Tokyo.

"Take these jewels and give them to your daughters when I die."

Her son took them in his large hands.

Her fingers were bare of any rings at all. She had grown too thin, and they had all slipped off.

She looked at her son from where she lay bedridden. His hairline had receded almost to the back of his head. He looked nothing like he once did, and this time she was the one too weak to leave her futon, not him.

His three daughters sat clustered together behind him, their heads bent and their bodies small, silently watching her. But his wife was not there. For she was due to give birth to her fourth child at any moment.

Her lips moved almost imperceptibly.

"Remember this . . ."

And then she fell silent. And then fell asleep.

Her son had no idea what she might have wanted to tell him not to forget. His hand held the jewels she'd given him; his fingers glittered with rings.

Long after this, I realized.

Perhaps she'd known all along.

Known that sometimes, no matter how much effort you make, it will all still end in failure and defeat. That what you've lost in the past can never truly return to you. But also, that from deep within these depths, precious stones may still emerge, glowing with their own light.

I'm the daughter of a jeweler. My eyes are hardly fooled!

She threw her money down as she spit the words, light-radiating jewels clutched in her other hand.

You presume to tell me *what is and isn't "really real"?*

Dr. Iimori's stones were produced in large quantities and sold in department stores everywhere. But a gemstone's value resides in its naturalness, and the man-made stones were generally shunned. Their production ceased in the 1990s, and today, there isn't even anyone left who properly remembers the process by which they were made.

But it was precisely these artificial stones that she yearned to hold in her hands.

I stand beside her bed, watching as life slips from her.

Watch as I turn to stone. As I turn into a jewel.

She dies. She is sixty-seven years old.

I look into her eyes. But they can no longer meet mine.

I understand for the first time that to die is to lose the ability to meet another's gaze.

♠

She lay in a wooden coffin dressed in white, the money she'd need to cross the Sanzu River into the Land of the Dead tucked into her breast pocket. The monk arrived and began to intone the sutras, and then both she and the coffin were placed in the incinerator and burned to ash.

New Year's Day had just passed, and the clouds hung low and heavy in the sky, light rain showers mixed with snow breaking out sporadically all day.

I looked up into the sky. The crematorium's smokestack stretched up toward the clouds. People's bodies turned to black smoke and rose up out of the smokestack to touch them.

The funeral director appeared, his white-gloved hands carrying long chopsticks and a box, and he began to put her scorched bones one by one into the box. As I watched him, I suddenly cried out involuntarily.

For glittering there amid the bones was a small diamond.

Since human bones are made of carbon, on rare occasions the intensity of the incineration forms small diamonds from them—the funeral director seemed completely unsurprised as he explained this to us.

Her son and her older sister used the chopsticks together to place this precious stone into the box. Her son's three daughters watched intently as they did.

And then I opened my eyes.

&

I stand in front of IMA. It is spring.

The tenth day of the Fourth Month has passed in Tokyo, the shade beneath the trees as they leaf out growing darker with each passing day, just as Izumi Shikibu observed a thousand years before—the world shining brighter than a dream even as the depth of human sorrow deepens.

I am making my way step-by-step down the stairs into the Ōedo subway line. People pass me on their way up the stairs into the light: one, then another, and then a third. I reach the landing and then walk down into a dim, unpopulated passage, eventually passing through the turnstile into the subway proper. I descend ever deeper into the earth.

The station announcements and the little song that plays when a train arrives echo off the tunnel walls. A still-new magenta-painted subway car pulls up to the platform. The car is nearly empty.

I enter the car. A rush of air from deep within the earth ruffles my hair. As it does, I hear a man's voice behind me.

"Are you waiting for someone to jump?"

The subway car gradually begins to move. The scene behind the glass before me slides away and disappears, replaced by darkness that reveals my reflection. A jewel hangs at my breast, glowing softly.

Slowly, I turn my head to look behind me.

HELLO MY BABY, HELLO MY HONEY

DULL PAIN ROSE from the pit of her stomach and flowed throughout her body, crashing over her only to ebb again, like a wave.

When she'd lost her virginity, the pain had been sharp, like a thick needle slid beneath a nail. This was a different sort of pain, less sharp, and it boiled up from deep within her, as if her uterus had been invaded by something that now spread outward to every part of her.

Ah-ah!

And then, the pain stopped.

Able to take a deep breath at last, she reached up to brush her sweat-soaked hair from where it stuck to her forehead and cheek. It tangled in her fingers.

Nevertheless, she was enfolded by a happiness she'd never felt before.

How long have I yearned for this?

For this child?

She found herself unexpectedly teary-eyed with joy.

It seemed she was on the verge of victory at last, after so many defeats.

Her mouth was dry and tasted of vomit.

The intervals between her contractions were shortening. She knew the next one would crash over her sooner than she thought.

She looked over at the window, but a black blanket had been hung over it, blocking any view of the outside world.

So quiet.

And then she heard it: the high-pitched buzz of a mosquito's wings, right next to her ear.

Her eyes flew open, and she sat up straight in her bed.

What now?

A mosquito, of all things—at a time like this?

She swatted the air around her.

She looked down and was confronted with the great swelling of her belly, and beyond that, her lower body totally exposed.

The mosquito was hovering above her pubic hair.

She remembered hearing long ago that only female mosquitoes drank blood. They needed it for when they gave birth—deprived of this special diet, they cannot have their children.

And indeed, the mosquito looked quite determined in its quest.

All at once, the buzzing stopped.

She looked down and saw that it had landed on her thigh.

The mosquito was speckled white and black. Its body, including its wings, undulated slowly.

She brought down her hand.

But the mosquito slipped through her fingers, flying straight up in the air.

Where is it? Where did it go?

She looked around, peering into space.

The buzzing suddenly rematerialized, right next to her ear.

She became frantic.

She batted the air with both hands.

The mosquito kept circling her.

Splat!

The sound echoed wetly.

She slowly opened her hand.

There were scattered black bits smeared across it, mixed with the vivid red of her own fresh blood.

It was summer, 1945.

She was, at that very moment, about to give birth.

◊

Old clothing and blankets had been readied in place of absorbent cotton. Looking at the pile, she remembered a woman who'd said to her, *If I'm going to die from a bomb dropped on me, I'd like to at least not have it be during my period!*

There were women whose menstruation had stopped by itself. But not her—she'd had to make sure she had cotton to absorb it every month. Which became a further humiliation once that cotton became rationed.

So when she stopped menstruating after getting pregnant, it had been a happy thing.

Less happy, though, was that ever since she'd gotten pregnant, she seemed to be hungry all the time.

When her younger sister had been pregnant, the smell of cooking rice had nauseated her so much she'd taken to her bed. And so she imagined that's how it would be for her too, that she would be stricken with morning sickness, constantly suppressing the urge to vomit.

But far from being unable to take food, she found she was mad with desire for it.

She looked back with fierce regret at all the times she'd left a piece of fat on her dish in the past—if only she'd eaten her fill when she'd had the chance!

She became unable to think of anything else.

Shameful.

But the truth was, her stomach was empty. Everyone—well, everyone who wasn't a soldier—was starving.

A potato field had been planted in front of the National Diet Building. People roasted rice bran to simulate chocolate.

She'd heard that in the gardens of Asaka-no-miya, Prince Yasuhiko's home in Shirokane, there lived an albino peacock—a gift from Germany or some such—but even it had ended up eaten. The long feathers of its tail, each one a lustrous, glossy white ending in an eye, were plucked from its body, its blood drained from its neck. Denuded of its glory, the peacock became just another piece of meat, roasted over fire.

A peacock, roasted.

Having thought this far, she realized she was salivating.

Even at this moment of extremity, she was still so hungry.

◊

Now, out beyond her swollen stomach, a small group of women had gathered. They peered as one into the area between her legs.

Blood had stuck here and there to her pubic hair and hardened.

A contraction crashed over her once again.

Ah-ah!

One of the women told her, from the far side of her splayed legs,

The baby is coming!

As if in answer, the surface of her enormous belly began to ripple and crawl.

Her skin grew hot as it stretched, her navel expanding wider and wider, her stomach seemingly about to split open.

Ah-ah!

It's about—it's about to happen!

Finally!

My child!

She was overcome with emotion. Tears streamed from her eyes.

Finally, an end to defeat.

How many people around me had died already?

Her brother.

Three of her cousins.

Her sister's daughter had lost her left eye.

Her father had written a note and left, never to be heard from again.

She had seen the streets on fire.

Firebombs had fallen from the sky with the snow. She'd stomped out the flames they brought, but still, in the end, her house had burned, too.

But now, finally—my child.

This child within me, born.

Like this bomb.

Its great flash of light, able to blow away an entire city.

This "uranium bomb."

It felt so hot between her legs, it was as if she burned too.

She'd first heard rumors of this new bomb the summer of the previous year.

A matchbox-sized piece of it could blow away an entire city.

It seemed that it wouldn't be long before this uranium bomb, with its new, terrible power, would be born.

It was her sister who passed along the rumor to her.

If only we had it, we could win the war right away!

Her sister was speaking quickly, her brows furrowed. Her bones stood out clearly where her dress opened at the collar.

Word at the time was that the Mariana Islands were surrounded by enemy warships. If Saipan were to fall, airstrikes on the Japanese mainland were likely to begin.

The farthest a bomber taking off from Chengdu could strike would be approximately Kyūshu. But if Saipan were to fall, the distance from the mainland would shorten and bombers could easily reach Tokyo.

Her sister's four-year-old son played behind her, swinging a stick like a sword.

Her sister looked over and watched him for a moment.

Tokyo—this is where I live, where my children live. I don't ever want bombs to drop down on us here.

As she listened to her sister's words, she noticed for the first time that there was a small gap between her two front teeth.

Her sister flatly concluded her thought.

So if that uranium bomb blows away the entire island of Saipan, so be it.

Listening to her sister, her eyes widened.

Uranium bomb.

She found herself drawn to it.

A matchbox-sized piece of it could blow away an entire city.

Could blow away London. Could blow away New York.

What sort of bomb was this?

How brilliant must its flash be?

Would the flames lick up red or blue?

Gripped with excitement, she leapt to her feet before she quite knew what she was doing.

When will it be born?

At that very moment, the stick wielded by her sister's son

swung through the air near her face, barely missing her eye, and ended up stabbing through the paper door behind her. It tore the panel, leaving paper hanging from the edges of the gaping hole ripped into it.

⟁

She knew as soon as she found out she was pregnant.

Her belly held light within it.

This new bomb—this special uranium bomb—was not something manufactured, but something born.

Years later, reading about the Manhattan Project—the US project to develop and test the world's first nuclear weapon—she had the strangest feeling come over her as she learned that the scientists themselves had thought the very same thing.

They had made bets.

Just before the bomb's birth.

Which would it be—boy or girl?

A dollar on boy.

A dollar on girl.

If the explosion was big, the bomb was a boy. If small, a girl.

And as for whether the bomb would be born at all?

This bet was ten dollars.

⟁

She was riding the waves of her contractions now, pushing with all her might as they ebbed and flowed.

Her thighs were wet with warm liquid.

Was it from her water breaking? Or was it blood? She couldn't tell.

Ah-ah!

The women reached their hands between her legs.

This being within me.

This child.

This bomb.

This light.

This Divine Wind . . .

She pushed and pushed.

She didn't even feel the pain anymore.

Only the heat between her legs.

She yearned for it—they all yearned for it to finally happen.

This birth.

She heard crying.

But it was not the cry of a child. It was the women, weeping.

She looked around.

The window was still covered with the black blanket. Somewhere out beyond it, she could hear the buzz of cicadas.

Defeat.

The war was lost.

The women were listening to a radio broadcast that kept cutting out.

It was so quiet.

The first thing a person does after being born is cry—but to do so as an adult?

She saw that a rush mat had been placed over her lower body for some reason. She felt blood still flowing from between her legs beneath it. Her thighs were smeared dark brown where it had dried.

She had an itch on her calf, and she raised her leg up to scratch it. Looking down, she saw a mosquito bite swelling red beneath her nails.

She also noticed that her own belly was no longer swollen.

She looked around once more.

She couldn't see what she'd given birth to—not anywhere.

All that was left was the reddish black of her afterbirth.

She soon found out that her hemorrhaging would continue for two weeks.

No Divine Wind in sight. No victory.

All that effort, all she had striven for until that day, the tenth of August—it had all been in vain.

She lay back on the bed and closed her eyes.

She felt herself dragged down by intense exhaustion into a heavy, deep sleep.

Even now, seventy-five years later, she seldom talked about it.

Which had it been, in the end?

What had I given birth to—or rather, failed to give birth to?

A boy?

A girl?

She could see the dazzling summer sun shining down on the verdant leaves of the trees outside her window.

It made her squint.

That summer had indeed witnessed the birth of a new bomb.

A bomb that truly could, with just a matchbox-sized piece of it, blow an entire city away.

Though people tended to compare it to other things—the size of an orange, the size of a pumpkin.

The American scientists had succeeded in their birth.

And the cities of Hiroshima and Nagasaki had been blown away.

All before she had even tried to birth her bomb.

Before it had a chance to blow Saipan away.

People burned.

Everything Japan had gathered to usher in its own birth—everything that might be related to it—was dismantled, thrown away, sunk to the bottom of Tokyo Bay. Though in truth, most of it had gone up in smoke already during the Tokyo carpet bombings.

She watched a woman walking in front a building under construction, supporting her swollen, pregnant belly as she passed.

She put her hand to her own flat belly.

The child in her belly had never come back to life. Her belly never held life within it again.

Her sadness had never lessened, not even a little.

But at the same time, somewhere in the recesses of her heart, she had found a certain peace.

That fearsome, beloved, yearned-for child.

That child that was never born.

Almost everyone had forgotten by now. Everyone but her.

And even she could no longer clearly remember the exact con-tours of the pain.

Though her stomach was still marked by the lines showing how it had stretched once, then shrunk again.

No matter how she washed or rubbed them, these would never disappear.

SEE

IT WAS THREE years ago that she turned sixty and lost her husband. It happened after years of caring for him, and at the funeral she laughed that she'd had enough of wiping his bottom so it was rather a relief; hearing this, worry began to worm its way into her two daughters' hearts. Though she seemed so resilient, her friends still offered her words of comfort telling her that when one of her daughters gave her a grandchild, she'd forget her troubles. But when her oldest did in fact give birth to a daughter, her heart seemed no lighter.

It was one month ago that she died in a car accident. Her oldest daughter rushed to the hospital, clutching her own daughter to her, and found her still barely conscious. By the time the younger arrived, she'd already passed.

What shocked everyone was that at the time of the accident, she'd been riding in the car of a man neither daughter knew. What's more, flowing from her corpse even more plentifully than blood was the choking scent of cheap perfume. The funeral parlor was flooded with its lingering stench.

◊

Sadako slowly blinks her eyes. Open or shut, all she sees is darkness. In darkness, a few minutes feels like a decade, a decade like a few minutes. She can't recall how long she's been like this.

But she remembers the coffee shop itself down to the smallest detail. She can see it with such clarity—every stain on the wall, every drop of condensation clinging to the water glass as she raises it to her lips to swallow the pill.

A man who says his name is Yamada sits before Sadako as she nervously pulls at the hem of her miniskirt. He's walking her through a stiltedly polite explanation of what he'd already explained to her in an email. Yamada's front teeth protrude slightly from between his lips, and he looks to be in his late twenties, around the same age as Sadako herself. Thinking of those teeth, Sadako is relieved that at the very least, her younger sister, Riko, isn't there to see her with this sort of man. If either she or her husband had had the slightest inkling she'd secretly signed up with Homerus, there's no way either would have agreed to take care of her daughter.

"Once you take the medication, in approximately ten minutes your vision will begin to cloud. After you've lost sight completely, your designated handler will arrive. Your handler will act as your guide and take you for your drive to the sea."

She'd seen photos online, of course, but this is the first time she's seen the bluish pill in person. It feels like a joke that a drug inducing blindness ended up with the name See.

See had caused quite a stir when it first came out. As one might expect, sex fiends used it in place of blindfolds in their play, and disability advocates proposed using it to raise awareness of the plight of the blind; still others predicted ways it could be used to commit crimes, recommending it be handled as a controlled substance. A religious sect sprang up advocating its use for enlightenment, explaining that it reveals the extent all of us are already blind. The truth of existence resides in darkness, they said, and only by letting go of sight can we see the world's true form.

A variety of businesses sprang up, ranging from sexual services to cafés to places using it to promote health and education, but this boom only lasted about a year; most endeavors ended up either prosecuted as illegal or simply going under. Homerus, along with a few others, managed nonetheless to continue, legally and quietly, after the initial craze died down.

"For your safety, cameras record the interior of the car and are monitored twenty-four hours a day, so rest assured that no matter what happens, our representatives can reach you immediately at any time. You will also be able to contact us easily if you begin to feel uncomfortable or nauseated; your handler will explain the exact method for doing so in the car. Blindness will last roughly three hours. You will remain securely within the car until your eyesight is fully restored. If you have any questions or concerns related to what I've just told you, please don't hesitate to ask."

Sadako recalls Yamada's words as she sits here now, alone in the dark. She remembers an article she'd read about a young woman who took See and never regained her sight. It's a side effect experienced by one out of every few million; there's no way of guaranteeing who might be that one. Unease begins to percolate in the darkness—bubbles that burst and disappear, only to be replaced by more. The table before her should have the coffee she'd been drinking still on it, the glass of water just to the side. But she has no way to confirm this, and she feels herself losing her grip on where in the world she might be. She reaches out her hand and touches the objects before her, but the moment her fingers leave them again, everything becomes once more uncertain.

Sadako finds her heart growing small, like a lost child's. She tries to commit to memory each moment she spends in darkness, but she realizes she doesn't know how to recall her experiences or put them in order if she can't see them.

How long does she wait before her handler arrives? It feels as if it could have been a very long time or almost no time at all.

"Pleased to meet you. My name is Jeremy."

The voice is low and resonant, the Japanese fluent. Normally, she would find it ridiculous to hear such a put-on, oh-so-Western moniker emerge from a Japanese face surely more suited to a name like Kenta Morita, but in her present state she finds the sound of it almost moving.

At Jeremy's cue, Sadako takes his hand, clings to it. Their fingers interlace. Unthinkingly, Sadako sighs, trembling slightly. How is it that in darkness, to come in contact with the hand or fingers or body of another, with another's warmth—how can this produce such comfort, and such excitement?

◊

Her two daughters were wearing cotton gloves. After the funeral, they'd decided to ready the house for sale immediately, and so they went straight away to clean it from stem to stern, if only to rid it of the smell of cheap perfume that lingered still in every room.

A business card fell all too easily from the drawer of the nightstand beside her pillow.

HOMERUS.

The word was embossed in gold letters across thick, glossy black paper.

Her younger daughter snatched up the card, indignation bursting through the mask she wore over her mouth.

"I wouldn't have bothered me if Mama had remarried or done whatever else she felt like, after all she was an adult—but this! This is too much!"

Homerus was a "date club" you joined in order to take a dose of See and let a man take you on a seaside drive. It had been a frequent topic of conversation in the tabloids and on various television shows, so both daughters recognized the name.

Her older daughter opened the doors of her dresser and with gloved hands began rifling through clothes that had, up till then, only been handled with utmost care with bare ones. She gave her sister a noncommittal reply.

"We shouldn't be mean about it. She must have been lonely after Papa died."

"You think it's a question of loneliness? First of all, why would she spend so much money on a thing like that? And did you see the picture of the guy who died in the accident with her? The police showed it to me and I almost fainted. If I'm going to end up dead like that, I'd like it to be with someone hot! At least that way, I'd be able to rest in peace."

"He was balding, I remember . . . but after all, Mama never actually saw him."

"That's even worse!"

Both daughters suddenly became silent, until it became too much and they began to giggle uncontrollably.

"Remember how panicked she got when she had cataracts and thought she was losing her sight? And now she's taking drugs to go blind for fun! Poor Papa."

Her younger daughter's mouth twisted in disapproval beneath her mask.

"He used to go to cabaret clubs, didn't he?"

Her older daughter's mouth twisted beneath her mask as well.

"He was young."

"Old people have desires too."

"Parents are different."

"And besides, men get old and eventually can't get it up anymore, but women can do it however old they get."

At that, her daughters grew silent once more, then looked at one another.

Each imagined, for one brief instant, their mother having sex, or rather, their mother as she must have been when having sex in the past. Both daughters were of course themselves the product of her having had sex with their father, but to actually imagine it was a rare and strange thing.

"What can you even do on a date like that if you can't see the sea? If only she hadn't done it, there wouldn't have been an accident, and she'd still be here now."

Her older daughter looked down at the double bed where no one would sleep again. She reached down with her gloved hand, picked up the Homerus card from where it had fallen, and slipped it into her pocket.

"We've reached the sea."

Jeremy's voice.

"The sea . . ."

Blinking in darkness, Sadako repeats the word to herself: *sea*. And as she does, she's overcome with the desire to reach out her hand, extend her fingers, and touch Jeremy's body, if only to confirm he was there.

"If you look to your right, you can see it now."

Sadako listens as hard as she can, as if to make sure not to miss the sound of his breath, the sound of his lips moving.

As she listens, the sun-drenched sea slowly spreads within

her. The morning had been cloudy, and it's autumn—the sea, if she could see it, would be the dirty gray Tokyo Bay, but instead it extends into the distance blue and endless just for her. She takes a deep breath. It's filled with an odor specific to the car's interior. Have they exited the highway? The car sways slightly side to side.

Sadako remembers making plans with her husband to rent a car and take a trip to the sea with their daughter. But with her mother's sudden death, their summer was taken up with planning the funeral and dealing with her house, so in the end they only got as far as the neighborhood pool. Sitting poolside wearing not a bikini but a one-piece due to the scar left by her cesarean, the person most annoyed by this development isn't her husband, isn't her daughter, but rather Sadako herself.

"Thanks to Mama dying, we never got to go to the sea and ended up here instead!"

Her daughter walks up, pool water dripping from her hair, and she holds out her tiny hand, her eyes shut tight. *C'mon, just one more!* Sadako draws a heart with her finger on her daughter's palm.

"A heart!"

Her daughter almost immediately demands *just one more* once more, pressing her little hand into Sadako's palm and screwing her eyes shut again.

Sadako's husband laughs ruefully as he drinks his beer.

"It's just the sea—we can always go next year."

Next year, next summer—when they finally arrive, will they really go? Her mother left so suddenly who's to say who might be missing in another year's time?

After all, none of them can see the future, not one single bit of it.

Sadako loses herself in her memories as if being pulled out by the tide.

The light of the sun in summer. Sadako in middle school, riding in the back seat with Riko. Her father at the wheel, her mother looking at a map spread out over her miniskirt.

Riko's small soft hand takes Sadako's, and she speaks, almost angrily.

"Your eyes are really shut, right?"

"They are, okay?"

Sadako makes a show of pressing her eyelids together. Behind them isn't darkness but rather the filtered light of the sun; she can see multicolored specks floating before her.

"What are you two doing?"

Her father's voice.

"We're playing Helen Keller!"

Riko's answer.

"You're playing what?"

Her mother's voice, from the passenger seat.

"We draw words on each other's hands, like *water* or whatever."

Riko tosses the explanation over her shoulder as she concentrates on drawing letters one by one across Sadako's palm.

There in darkness, everything is given a name. The cold liquid emerging from a well becomes W-A-T-E-R. The feel of someone's touch playing across her palm. A fingertip tells her the name of each and every thing around her, one by one by one.

Sadako focuses her attention on the palm of her hand.

S

E

A

Sea. The sea.

Sadako slowly opens her eyes.

What was it that Riko actually wrote on her palm all those years ago?

To her right, she can see the sea.

Her father takes a hand from the wheel and rolls down the window.

"The sea!"

A gust of wind blows in and makes the map in her mother's lap dance.

Riko, in a bored tone of voice, whispers in her sister's ear.

"I wanna go home. First of all, I hate the car, it makes me sick. This is the worst, the absolute pits!"

Riko doesn't even glance at the sea and instead thrusts her left hand at Sadako, her eyes shut so tight there's a crease between her brows. The light from the sun shines in through the window, dancing back and forth across her palm. Their mother, laughing, turns slowly to look at them. Small hairs escaping from the single braid she's pulled her hair back into dance back and forth in the light. But Sadako cannot recall her mother's face as it must have looked when she was that young.

⟨⟩

Sadako made sure she was completely alone, then slipped the Homerus card from her pocket. She lightly traced the ridges of the embossed letters with her fingertip. In the end, she sent a message to the email address listed on the card.

If Riko ever found out that Sadako had sent a message to the email address on the card, she'd surely never agree to take care of her daughter again.

❧

She hears the sound of Jeremy pressing a switch, then feels the wind as it comes in through the window. It smells of the sea.

Sadako takes a deep breath and blinks in darkness. Finally, unable to stand it any longer, she lifts her right hand from where it's been resting—the point where her leg emerges from her miniskirt—and slowly extends it in Jeremy's direction. It wanders, suspended in space. But soon enough it's enfolded in the warmth of Jeremy's left hand. Their fingers interlace. From time to time a gust of wind blows in, making the tiny hairs escaping from the single braid she's pulled her hair back into dance back and forth.

Sadako brings Jeremy's left hand slowly down to rest upon her knee, opening it up so she can caress its palm with both hands.

"My daughter likes to play a game called Helen Keller. Someone draws pictures or letters on your palm, and you have to guess what they are."

Sadako uses her hands to open out Jeremy's palm.

Sadako touches it with her fingertip. Jeremy, ticklish, begins to laugh. Which makes Sadako laugh too.

When was the last time she laughed like this?

Sadako takes another deep breath. This time, stronger than the smell of the sea is the smell of her own perfume.

Sadako begins to slowly trace a letter across Jeremy's palm.

S—

Sadako blinks as her fingertip begins to trace the next letter across his palm; at that exact moment, something shakes her violently. Something's hit them. In the dark, the moment stretches out into infinity. She hears the sound of brakes, the sound of impact. Jeremy! Where are you?

No, the man next to her, he has a different name. Andrew? Tony? No, that's right, it's John. How many times has she done this, tracing letters across someone's palm? Tens? Hundreds?

Here in darkness, she can't recall how much time has passed since she went for her first drive with Jeremy to the sea. She feels herself slowly moving farther and farther away from that hand, that body, those fingers, that name. She extends her fingers, trying to grasp something, anything, and ends up touching something gooey and warm. The sound of a siren rings out as her consciousness fades.

"Mama! Mama!"

She had no idea how much time had passed while in darkness. It wasn't Sadako who was calling for her mama. It was Sadako who was being called. Searching through her memory, her eyes still firmly shut, Sadako vaguely recalled that she was no longer a daughter; she was now a mother.

Summer. At some point had they finally gone to see the sea?

"Mama!"

When had she stopped being a daughter? She still felt like she'd felt back then, in her twenties. When had she gotten so old?

"Mama, please! Open your eyes!"

The voice of the daughter to whom she'd given birth. But she was afraid to open her eyes. When had her daughter given birth to a daughter of her own?

Her ears picked up the conversation of some people passing by.

"Do you smell that perfume! It's awful!"

She had the feeling that, open or shut, her eyes would see nothing.

So instead of her eyelids, she slowly opened her palm. And waited, longingly, for the touch of a fingertip.

COCO'S CENTURY

HER NAME WAS Ko.

That's it—just the single character: 子. Ko.

Most people thought it was a mistake, or missing something.

She was the second daughter of Yoki, who had married into the family from the neighboring village one evening at sixteen years old, under the full moon. Yoki's mother, Ko's grandmother, was called Kon, so it was simple to take away the *n* and make Ko.

Ko.

Ko hated the name Ko.

It always made her feel that she was missing something.

It was hard to call her just Ko, so people began occasionally calling her Ko-Ko.

Ko-Ko? Okay, that'll be three slices for three sen, five rin.

Out there in that snowbound Niigata village, no one had ever heard of Coco Chanel—the only thing that came to mind for them was Ko-Ko brand pickled radish.

Her sister's name was also a single character: 操. Misao.

But this single character gave her three syllables—*Mi-sa-o*—where Ko got only one. But in exchange, Misao was missing her right eye.

There were competing accounts of why—that a clipped fingernail had fallen onto her face as a baby and worked its way into the corner of her eye, or that she had contracted encephalitis, or that she'd simply fallen and hit her head—but no one seemed to know the real reason.

What was sure was that her right eye had always been clouded over, the lid permanently sunken in.

In any case, Ko's mother frequently charged Ko with taking care of Misao, despite Misao being older. She took on the mission with her life.

Yer sis's nuh aye, ta per wee ting.

People would say this to her in their thick Niigata dialect, but when Ko would tell the story later, she'd translate to standard Tokyo speech.

So sorry about your sister's eye, the poor little thing.

Once, on the way back from elementary school, Misao fell in a hole.

A group of boys gathered, calling meanly after her, *Blind bat, blind bat!*

Ko helped Misao out of the hole, her body shaking with rage.

She took careful note of each and every one of the boys who had made fun of Misao, writing down their names and cursing them: *Die!*

And indeed, each and every one of those boys was drafted into the military during the war and died.

But Ko, for her part, never forgot those boys even after their deaths, and never forgave them, either.

She would say to herself—

Serves you right!

Ko left for Tokyo at age sixteen.

She had still yet to hear the name Coco Chanel, but nonetheless she ended up working as a seamstress at a glitzy department store on the Ginza.

She had always been good at sewing.

She used the money from her first paycheck to buy a gift for Misao: a glass eye.

She used the money from her second paycheck to buy a ticket for Misao to visit her in Tokyo, have the glass eye placed in her socket, dress her up in a beautiful kimono, and have her portrait taken to give to a matchmaker to find her a husband.

This was the only time Misao ever wore the glass eye.

She claimed it was a bother to slip her eye in and out of her face all the time, and she placed it instead in the back of the drawer in her vanity for safekeeping.

Naturally, she also regarded going to find a husband to be an unnecessary bother as well.

Ko resented her sister greatly for this, but Misao didn't care.

Many years after, Misao collided with a man while skiing, and that's who she ended up marrying.

Ko lived alone in Tokyo, working diligently.

The other seamstresses made fun of her Niigata accent. She had a hard time differentiating her *i*'s from her *e*'s.

Ko tried her hardest to adopt the Tokyo dialect, and she washed her face many times a day. If you washed your face with Tokyo water, they said, you'd end up with a Tokyo face.

But finally, Ko ended up fleeing the department store.

Ko, unable to make her name in the industry like Coco Chanel did, wanted to return to her hometown.

To that little snowbound village, where her mother was, where Misao was.

To that house with the grass-thatched roof, where her ancestors slumbered in the garden beneath the grand stone, shaded by the largest Japanese cedar in the village.

To when Ko was a child, was Ko.

But there was nowhere for Ko to return to.

That village, that house, had no use for a second-born daughter come home.

Eventually, through family connections, Ko was offered a job in Niigata as a live-in maid.

She was taken to a modern redbrick building standing at the corner of the street.

It was Seika Girls High School.

Ko was taken into the building and introduced to the principal, Magoya Katsuda, a historian of the Meiji Restoration descended of former samurai, and his two daughters, Michi and Tetsuko, who worked there as teachers.

Ko was dazzled by the sight of them.

Michi, the older sister, wore a gorgeously patterned kimono, while Tetsuko, the younger, was decked out in a Western-style dress and high heels.

To Ko, they seemed like emissaries from another world.

When Michi bought a kimono at the department store, she would buy all the other kimonos of the same pattern too. For she couldn't stand to have another woman in town wearing the same thing.

Tetsuko had returned from university in America speaking English. Not only that, she had a boyfriend. His name was Kiyoshi, and he was tall and had blue eyes (for his father was an Englishman).

To Michi and Tetsuko, Ko seemed like an emissary from another world as well.

Nonetheless, Ko enjoyed the job, and she worked hard, sometimes getting a chance to show off her sewing skills. She also sometimes helped with classes.

So when Ko mentioned that she was off to meet with a matchmaker to find a husband, Michi and Tetsuko broke into tears.

We don't want you to go! Can't you stay here forever?

In the end, Ko did get married and did quit her job, but the bond between the women would last their whole lives.

Michi eventually took over for her father and became the

principal of the school, while Tetsuko translated Laura Ingalls Wilder novels—*These Happy Golden Years*, *Little House in the Big Woods*, and so on.

Ko received the translations as a gift from Tetsuko and displayed them proudly next to her television. Having attended only elementary school in her life, however, Ko was never able to read them herself.

> *"As Laura floundered on, plunging into the deep snow, she suddenly laughed aloud.*
> *'Well!' she thought. 'Here I am. I dread to go on, and I would not go back.'"*

Ko was twenty-four when she got married.

Her husband worked at a store making traditional Japanese sweets.

Michi and Tetsuko sent an enormous vanity with a beautiful mirror attached to it as a wedding present. Its extravagance looked out of place in their modest, tatami-floored apartment.

Her husband's store was on the Ginza, but as wartime continued, sugar became scarce, and he eventually ended up working for the company that managed the building.

It didn't matter to Ko one way or the other if her husband made sweets or managed a building.

What mattered to her was having a baby.

Her name was Ko—子—after all. Child.

She dreamed of the day she'd have a child of her own to hold in her arms.

All three of her brothers had gone off to war.

Both Ko and Misao had returned to the countryside to see them off, waving Japanese flags with red suns in their centers and taking photographs.

Ko's husband was eventually pressed into service at an army munitions factory. He developed pneumonia from breathing the gunpowder and died soon after he returned.

All three of her brothers were sent to the front in Siberia, but they did not die there.

The old house, too, remained unburned.

Finally, the war ended.

But Ko still did not have a child.

So she decided to adopt one.

Ko's adopted daughter was a child with dark, thick eyebrows.

A child who became my mother.

In other words, Ko is my grandmother.

At last, Ko was no longer Ko, the child, but now Mother, and then Grandmother.

When she would put me to sleep as a little girl, Ko would tell me her story.

When her husband died, Ko took the money she inherited and went for her first trip overseas—a tour around the world.

She went everywhere: to Hawaii, to Shanghai, to London, to Cairo, to New York City.

In a duty-free shop in Paris, she treated herself to a tiny bottle of perfume made by Coco Chanel. She hid it away in her vanity when she returned home, for safekeeping.

She was no longer pickle-smelling Ko-Ko. She was Coco, and she smelled of the finest perfume.

Her hair was streaked with white, and she took to putting white netting around the short, permed curls.

Her heavy breasts hung from her chest.

Once she turned eighty-five, she began to forget things.

First it was her bankbook. Then her signatory stamp. Her handbag. The house keys.

One memory, then another, would just disappear.

She lost the ability to do the sewing she was so good at, and eventually the ability to cook. She began to subsist on a diet of only the sweet white bread sold in supermarkets.

The television had become a black lump. It had been a long time since *Little House on the Prairie* had stopped airing. The books remained in their pride of place beside it, though.

Soon Ko had to be put in a nursing home for the elderly.

In the end, she suffered multiple strokes and had to be hospitalized.

By then, she had forgotten nearly everything.

One day when I was visiting her, she turned to me and asked me a question, a serious expression on her face.

Someone visits me who says I'm her mother.

But did I really have a child?

I don't remember that at all, no matter how hard I try.

Ko had both her arms strapped to the bed, and the IV made purple bruises where it entered her body. She would forget almost immediately about the IVs once they were put in and tear out the needles again and again.

Ko had stopped talking about her days as Ko, the child.

Yet still she continued to live.

Lying there on the white sheets of the hospital bed.

Her eyes wide, staring at the ceiling.

It bothered me, and I started visiting her less and less.

She was ninety-nine years old when she died.

Misao had died seven years before, but Ko had not been able to attend the funeral.

And after all was said and done, where had that glass eye ended up?

Sleeping here next to my own daughter, now two years old, I think sometimes about Ko.

Ko, my grandmother unconnected by blood.

I realize with a start that she would have been one hundred years old right now, had she lived.

There were so many things I should have asked her, but now it's too late.

My daughter splays out on the bed next to me, her breathing growing regular as she falls asleep.

I lean over and begin to tell her a story.

The story of Coco.

The story of Ko.

SHE WAITED

1936

There, in the little town where the narrow Silberstraße ran
straight through, starting at the church on the hill,
she looked up.
A ladder leaned against the stone wall beneath the red
  domed roof of a building
where the Olympic emblem was being carved into the
  stone:

five rings and the word OLYMPIA, and between them the
 date:
1936.

This was Czechoslovakia, formerly Bohemia,
a place called Sankt Joachimsthal—Saint Joachim's
 Valley.
She waited—
for the Olympics,
for the sacred fire to come to her little town,
for the fire, for its light, to illuminate her little town.

There's a reason this narrow road is called the
 Silberstraße.
In the sixteenth century, in Saint Joachim's Valley, *silver*
 first emerged—
over five thousand men arrived, ready to get rich quick—
from Saxony, in Germany—
they came and dug deep into the earth.
The silver was minted into coins that spread all across
 Bohemia,
coins called *Joachimsthalers,* or *thalers* for short.
They eventually reached even the New World, as *dollars*—
for this is the origin of the dollar.

Torch in hand, men descended into darkness,
excavating deep into the earth,
but as they dug, less and less silver emerged
replaced by more and more mysterious shiny black stone.

Among the men, a mysterious disease began to spread—
their bodies grew sluggish and would bleed without
    stopping—
and so they began to call the shiny black stone *pitchblende*,
German for *accursed stone.*

In the eighteenth century, a new element was discovered
    within this *accursed stone.*
It was given the name *uranium*, after the planet Uranus.
When uranium is mixed with glass, it glows fluorescent
    green under ultraviolet light.
Soon uranium glass spread all throughout Europe.

It was prized by the aristocracy, made into wine glasses,
    vases, necklaces,
even instruments for irrigating the eye.
According to Greek myth, Uranus, the sky god,
was born to the earth goddess Gaia despite her virginity,
and when mother and son made love,
the world was visited by darkness.

At the same time she was looking up at the Olympic
    emblem being carved into the wall,
eleven virgins had gathered
in Greece, at the ruins of the Temple of Hera at Olympia,
all dressed in white.
During the ceremony, the virgins gathered the light of the
    sun using mirrors.
It was July 20th, the first time the sacred fire relay took place.

The flame was resurrected, the sacred fire passed from
    torch to torch—
the fire stolen from the sun and given to humanity by
    Prometheus—
from Greece, the Land of Olympia, to Berlin, in Nazi
    Germany—
to the Olympic Stadium, where the Opening Ceremony
    took place, led by Adolf Hitler.
It took twelve days to make the journey.
3,308 runners carried the torch,
the flame passing hand to hand, bringing its light.
And she waited—
for the sacred fire to come to her little town,
for the fire, for its light, to illuminate her little town.

Finally, at one in the morning on July 31st, the sacred fire
    reached Prague,
and then at 4:30 a.m. reached Straskov, then Terezín at
    6:15, then Teplice at 9:00—
but the sacred fire never reached the little town.

1938

It was two years after the Berlin Olympics.
The Nazi army invaded the area as if following the sacred
    fire's path,

their tanks made by Krupp, the same company that
    manufactured the torch itself—
the flames burned all in their path to ashes.
The Nazi army arrived in the little town the sacred fire
    never reached.

Torch in hand, men descended into darkness
excavating deep into the earth,
but instead of miners, now it was prisoners of war brought
    by the Nazis who mined the *accursed stone*.

In the center of a big city filled with brand-new buildings
thrown up under the banner of reconstruction following
    an earthquake's devastation,
she looked up.
Flags with red suns in their center joined flags bearing the
    Olympic emblem,
flying as far as the eye could see.
On the posters showing Mount Fuji and the Olympic
    rings in gold,
letters spelling TOKYO were set beside numbers spelling
    out the year:
1940.
It was the 2600th Anniversary of the Founding of Japan,
and this was Tokyo, the Imperial Capital of the Empire of
    Japan.
She waited—
for the Olympics,

SHE WAITED

for the sacred fire to come to her city,
for the fire, for its light, to illuminate everything around her.

1940

It was four years after the Berlin Olympics.
The fire of Olympia, Prometheus's gift, was to be borne
    from Greece this time to the Far East,
to the stadium where the Opening Ceremony would
    occur in Tokyo,
the capital of the Japanese Empire.
It was to be a grand Olympic relay to bring the sacred fire
    from
Olympia to Athens, then Istanbul, Ankara, Tehran,
    Kabul, Peshawar, Delhi, Kolkata, Hanoi,
Guangdong, Tianjin, Seoul, Busan . . .
The flame was to be borne by men on foot and horseback,
its light crossing Eurasia eastward hand to hand until it
    reached the Land of the Rising Sun.
Would the Latin phrase *ex oriente lux* end up being
    changed to *ex occidente lux*?

She looked up at the flags with suns in their centers,
but they were no longer accompanied by those with the
    Olympic emblem.
All that passed by her were parade floats for the 2600th
    Anniversary of the Founding of Japan.

It was November 10th.
The streets were dim, the lights shut off by government
    decree to conserve power.
She waited—
for the Olympics,
for the sacred fire to come to her city,
for the fire, for its light, to illuminate everything around
    her.

But the Olympics were never held,
all the men were sent to the battlefield,
and the sacred fire never reached her.

1941

It was one year after the Tokyo Olympics failed to
    happen.
The Japanese Imperial Army not only retraced the path of
    the torch relay that was never run,
but went east as well,
borne by bombers rather than horses, flames burning all
    in their path to ashes,
attacking America, bombing Pearl Harbor in Hawaii:
the Second World War had begun.

Torch in hand, men descended into darkness
excavating deep into the earth.

The nuclei of uranium atoms could now be split,
and the energy produced could create the greatest bombs
    the world had ever seen—
bombs that we now call nuclear weapons:
10 kilograms of Uranium-235 were needed to make one.
A top secret nuclear weapon development plan called the
    Ni-Go Project was begun,
a collaboration between physicists at the National
    Institute of Physical and Chemical Research and the
    Japanese Imperial Army.
A plan was hatched to transport large amounts of
    uranium
from Nazi Germany to its ally, the Japanese Empire.
Accursed stone was transported by rail from Saint Joachim's
    Valley to the outskirts of Berlin,
where uranium was extracted from it and taken to Kiel
    Bay—
passed hand to hand, it was placed in a submarine to be
    transported along the Atlantic Ocean floor,
bound for the Land of the Rising Sun.

1945

Kiel Bay, where the yacht races of the Berlin Olympics
    had been held,
back when the sacred fire illuminated the nation,
was once more illuminated by flames.

The naval base, the town hall, the church of Saint
    Nikolai, the opera house—all were on fire.
The submarines known as U-boats were anchored in the
    bay. They were called Grey Wolves.
One bore forty-seven brown packages of uranium.
The U-boat's number was only one off from that of the
    uranium within it: U-234.
Two men from the Empire of Japan accompanied the men
    from Nazi Germany on the U-boat
to take the uranium east.

She waited.
In the streets of Tokyo, where the Olympics had failed to
    come,
where the sacred fire had failed to reach,
she looked up at the dark sky.
Rumors repeated:
the scientists of this great country were making a bomb
    more powerful than any ever seen before,
a bomb called a *uranium bomb*—
a matchbox-sized piece would be enough to bathe the
    streets of New York in flames.
Torch in hand, men descended into darkness.
Bearing its uranium cargo, the U-boat crossed the ocean
    floor.
As it headed south across the Atlantic, a coded message
    was received:
Nazi Germany had unconditionally surrendered.

But even if Germany had fallen, the Empire of Japan had
   not!
The two Japanese men onboard the submarine insisted in
   fluent German:
If this uranium is delivered, the bomb can be created—
it can be created and used and the war can still be won!
The target would be Saipan—
if Saipan were taken out, the distance would be too great
   for the Allied planes
and land war would be avoided!
But it was decided to surrender the submarine to the
   Americans
and the two Japanese men swallowed Luminal,
collapsing into a heap on a bed, snoring unnaturally,
the white bedsheets soaked in black diesel.
The black flags announcing defeat were hung from the
   periscope once the U-boat had surfaced
while the bodies of the Japanese men sank to the floor of
   night-dark sea.

She waited.
The Tokyo streets were now illuminated, bathed in flames.
The air raids of the land war had begun.
And she waited—
but the uranium failed to reach her,
and the bomb was never completed.
The bomb she'd so anticipated ended up dropped on Japan
   instead—

bombs named Little Boy and Fat Man,
illuminating everything around them as they burned
     everyone to ashes.
The war ended,
but her life, their lives, did not.
Torch in hand, men descended into darkness.

SHEDDING

1. TABLE

She took a deep breath in the science classroom; it tasted of dust and chemicals. A human skeleton hung beside the blackboard. The shelf next to it held beakers, droppers, and flasks, and farther back, a locked cabinet held glass bottles of various fluids: chloric acid, mercury, hydrogen peroxide, ethanol.

Mitsuko had dreamed of this from childhood—of having a lab of her own, mixing substances together, determining their mass, heating them up in flasks, recording chemical reactions.

When she'd become the science teacher at a private girls' high school, her dream had come true.

Hundreds of girls must have passed through this room in the fifteen years she'd taught here. Their numbers had dwindled lately, but the cherries had begun to bloom last month just like always, heralding the graduation of another class of third-year students. Only Mitsuko remained, preparing once more to teach the same things to yet another group of students.

Mitsuko was approaching forty now, and she knew every nook and cranny of this room like the back of her hand. She could mentally catalog its contents without trying—the condition of each Bunsen burner, the size of each flask, the name of each substance in the locked cabinet: zinc, aluminum, ammonia, sulfur . . .

Water is known as H_2O. Two atoms of hydrogen and one of oxygen.

Every substance on earth is made of various combinations of elements.

When young Mitsuko learned that for the first time, it revolutionized her world. As much as when Helen Keller made the connection between the substance running over her hand and the word *water.*

Helen Keller became able, with her own hand, to hold *water.* And Mitsuko became able, with her own hand, to hold *H_2O.*

One learns, one by one, the names of things. And then, one by one, that of the elements composing them.

One holds things by their name.

This is grass. That is a spoon. This is a human.

Grass contains silica—SiO_2.

A spoon is an alloy combining iron—Fe—with chrome—Cr.

A human body is oxygen (O), carbon (C), hydrogen (H), nitrogen (N), calcium (Ca), phosphorus (P) . . .

And thus, Mitsuko could hold each one in her hand—each blade of grass, each spoon, each person.

✦

Standing there at the front of the science classroom, now filled with rows of students looking at her from behind the masks on their faces, Mitsuko, a mask secured to her face as well, pointed at the periodic table hanging on the wall behind her, saying:

"Harry's heart liebt Berlin butterflies!

"H is for hydrogen, He for helium, Li for lithium, Be for beryllium, B for boron. *Liebt* is German for *loves*. Sentences like this can help you remember the order of the elements on the periodic table.

"The periodic table was invented by a Russian scientist named Dmitri Mendeleev in the late nineteenth century. If you memorize the table and the atomic numbers of each element on it, you can predict chemical reactions.

"That's right—just by understanding the periodic table, anyone can predict future results before they happen!

"Amazing, don't you think?"

She couldn't keep her eyes from straying to the seats among the rows that stood conspicuously empty.

The number of chairs and desks were set in each classroom, the science classroom shared between school years even as the number of seats in the room remained the same.

A student had been lost last year as well.

Her students sat in their chairs in their reddish-brown blazers and skirts, blue ribbons tied in bows upon their breasts. They were talking amongst themselves through masks covering the lower halves of their faces—masks of unwoven cloth, polyurethane masks, masks with lamé threaded through the material, masks of every color imaginable. She'd heard there were schools considering adding regulations to their dress codes that would permit only masks of plain white cloth.

"Quiet please! Quiet!"

Mitsuko's voice as she raised it was muffled by her mask. It was made of white unwoven cloth that had a heat-conserving property.

For a brief moment, the classroom quieted.

Silence reigned.

But the moment passed, and the students began talking softly to each other again.

The classroom filled once more with restive murmurs.

Nothing in life is to be feared, it is only to be understood.

It was the scientist Marie Curie who said that.

Wasn't it?

Class was over, and Mitsuko, alone again in the empty classroom, reached into the pocket of her white skirt and withdrew her phone.

An app appeared on the screen.

My Period Calendar.

This was the thirteenth time she'd checked it since morning.

Decorated with pink flowers and hearts, the app recorded the frequency of the user's menstrual cycle, tracking ovulation, body temperature, and so on.

When Mitsuko heard the English word *period*, she immediately thought of the periodic table in her classroom, but apparently it could also refer to menstruation.

A week's time—168 hours, to be exact—was about to pass since the day she'd normally have her period. Three years, four months, and five days had passed since she began going to the hospital alone for fertility treatments, hoping to get pregnant. She had undergone hormone therapy, donated extra embryos, received in vitro fertilization with donated sperm. It seemed that now, finally, this long period of effort was about to pay off.

Mitsuko was single, but she wanted to have a baby.

Truth be told, she even felt it to be a kind of duty.

Every day she stood before her class, facing more and more empty seats, absences she felt increasingly compelled to fill.

Like a bee in a broken hive—indeed, what compels the male worker bees to excrete honey from their abdomens is the desire to reconstruct the missing pieces of their world.

She poured as much money as she could into the effort.

Lacking a spouse or partner, she was ineligible for government support, but at the very least, in vitro fertilization was much simpler a process these days than it had been before. Still, her salary was hardly high, and she ended up going through all her savings as well.

All that spent money, all that shed blood—dark blood smeared on sanitary napkins, on toilet bowls, on silver forceps, on absorbent cotton—her heart beat fast at the thought of it all.

At any rate, she needed to calm down.

Whenever she needed to calm down, Mitsuko would think of history's greatest scientists.

For example, Pierre and Marie Curie.

The Nobel-winning Curies—Marie even winning two, one for physics and one for chemistry!

They put so much effort into their discovery of the radioactive element radium. They imported a total of eleven tons of uranium ore from the mountains of Bohemia all the way to Paris, using up the pittance they earned through teaching and three long years of working every day to do so. They gave everything they had to the effort.

The two of them never wavered in their faith in their endeavor.

In the end, they succeeded in extracting 0.1 grams of radioactive radium from the eleven tons of ore.

Radioactive radium that glowed blue-white, like a fairy light, in the dark.

They say that Marie called it "my child, radium," and kept it beside her pillow as she slept.

This is the kind of resilience it takes to truly conduct research, and to succeed.

And at the end of it all, what did they achieve? A historic discovery and worldwide fame.

◊

Just as Mitsuko was leaving the science classroom to return to the teacher's lounge, her phone began to vibrate. She slid her hand into the skirt pocket at her hip and pulled it out.

Her younger sister had sent her a LINE message.

It was a sticker showing boy band members made into cartoons.

The subject line read simply "♡ Thank you ♡."

The message momentarily struck Mitsuko as rather cryptic, but then she remembered that her sister had yet to return the funeral clothing she'd lent her about a month ago, and figured it must be about that.

Thrifty by nature, her sister had made a point of coming to her house to borrow them. It seemed she figured it would be a waste to buy new funeral clothes just because she'd gained weight post-pregnancy and could no longer fit into what she'd worn for their parents' funerals.

It was true that Mitsuko had always been a bit fatter than her sister, but it hurt a bit to think it was to the same extent as post-birth weight gain, and in her heart of hearts she wished her sister would just go buy something, no matter how cheap or inelegant—in the end, though, she didn't have much choice but to go along with her plan.

Her sister's former supervisor at the travel agency where she used to work had died, so it was for his funeral that she needed the clothing.

"He was a sex pest at work, actually, and I remember wishing sometimes he would just die." Her sister, with her brown-dyed hair and her black polyurethane mask, was stuffing the funeral clothes still in their plastic dry cleaning bag into another bag, this one of blue polypropylene, as she said this. "Little did I imagine he really would!"

It was this supervisor's fault, in fact, that she hadn't been able to take her maternity leave even a month before the due date, and he'd made her work overtime as well. It had been a difficult birth, but the baby turned out to be healthy, and both mother and child were celebrated for their achievement. The hospital even thanked her for delivering a healthy baby during such difficult times. Nonetheless, for some reason—not enough tax money or manpower or something—she wasn't able to find childcare, and this supervisor didn't allow her to extend her maternity leave, either, so she ended up having to quit her job completely.

It seemed not the worst thing in the world to have wished death on such a man.

"But still," she continued, "it really gets on my nerves that now that he's actually dead, I have to go pay my respects—even bring a funeral offering! Though I guess if he did me the favor of dying, I can't very well skip the funeral."

Her sister snorted in laughter beneath her mask. "Too bad he couldn't have kicked the bucket nearer to when someone else did so I could save on dry cleaning, though," she said, spitting the words out.

He did me the favor of dying.

As she listened to her sister, Mitsuko thought about how illogical it was that we commemorate the deaths of the worst and the best among us the same way.

If this is about the funeral clothes, you can just send them.

She didn't really think her sister would willingly pay the delivery fee, of course.

Her sister's apartment building was only two stops away, but Mitsuko nonetheless tried to take care of everything with her via

LINE. This was partly because she was tired of hearing her sister, who was now working part-time as a homecare helper on top of raising her child, complain. Her sister recently learned that the grandchild of one of her clients was a student of Mitsuko's, giving her even more reason to go out of her way to tell Mitsuko about every little thing that happened.

Time passed, but the LINE message remained UNREAD. Mitsuko stuffed her phone back in her pocket without waiting for it to change to READ.

The students had almost all left for home, and the school's halls resounded with silence.

She glanced around the stairwell and caught sight of a tiny ant writhing in a corner, covered in dust.

Returning to the teacher's lounge, Mitsuko saw two third-year teachers wearing cotton masks with elastic ear loops talking quietly, their demeanors grave. One of the third-year students had failed to return to school since the beginning of the new year—that's what they must be talking about.

She packed up her things to go home, then threw her jade-green spring coat over her shoulders and walked straight to the restroom.

She passed quickly by the sinks and hurried into the farthest stall to the left. She pulled her leggings and underwear down in one motion and sat down on the toilet.

Reaching into her bag, she withdrew a plastic-wrapped package and then hurriedly unwrapped it. The pink pregnancy test inside was shaped like a digital thermometer.

Mitsuko carefully slid the test between her legs. And then, as if beginning to pray, she began to urinate. She shifted her hips occasionally to prevent the urine from touching her hand.

As she urinated, she suddenly remembered that she'd forgotten to lock the science classroom.

Her mood, which had been rather elevated, now fell to earth with a crash. She watched as a small fly walking across the sanitary napkin disposal box beside her interrupted its progress and just sat there, perfectly still.

The students said the science classroom was cursed. They seemed to seriously believe it.

They said it was the curse's fault that Mitsuko couldn't seem to bring her pregnancies to term, miscarrying twice. Starting about a month ago, things had reached the point that students whose contraception had failed began sneaking into the classroom in hopes the curse would prevent their pregnancies.

So Mitsuko had started making it a point to be sure the classroom door was always locked when she left.

After all, it was dangerous—there were Bunsen burners and alcohol lamps in there. And it grated on her to think that people driven by illogic were invading a room of science.

Mitsuko thought about this as she continued to urinate.

Curses were neither here nor there, but she preferred to maintain certain standards of precision and accuracy in all things.

After all, she hadn't miscarried twice; she'd miscarried three times.

The dribbling sounds of her urination continued for a while, then finally stopped.

She withdrew the pregnancy test from beneath her and looked into the little window.

Would the pink lines appear?

Three minutes stretched before her like an eternity.

2. PUNCTUATION MARK

Every English sentence ends in a punctuation mark, usually a period.

Back when Tokino worked as an English-language typist, she would tap the period key with her right ring finger.

Lying there in her flower-patterned organic cotton mask, staring at the stains on the ceiling, she reflected that she would like to use that finger now to put a period at the end of her life.

She'd been having this thought again and again for five months, ever since she was struck by a cerebral hemorrhage that paralyzed the left side of her body. There were several states in the United States that had legalized euthanasia, she knew; alternatively, perhaps she could go to Switzerland.

Though that would take effort, and money.

Her sigh filled her mask with humidity.

If only this hadn't happened, she'd be reaching the end of another productive day: she'd have cleaned her room from stem to stern, prepared the rice, performed her English typing tasks, finished her preparations for dinner . . .

Tokino had already raised her daughter and taken care of her father-in-law and then her husband until both had passed away. When her daughter divorced and returned home with her infant daughter, she'd helped raise her grandchild as well. She'd lived her life working for others, devoting herself to them, and she'd received their appreciation in return.

But now she couldn't clean, couldn't cook, couldn't do the laundry, couldn't type. Even going to the bathroom by herself was beyond her.

As she lay there counting up the things she could no longer do, she began to realize she was a help to no one, that her very existence must be a nuisance to everyone around her. She experienced a great feeling of emptiness at the realization.

She knew that since her collapse, her daughter left work much earlier than before to take care of her, and that her granddaughter had to cut back on her cram school classes as well.

Tokino kept her silence, and her newspaper and reading glasses remained where they'd been placed by her pillow.

But it was only now that this silence would be tolerated. If she kept quiet when her daughter was around, she'd find herself the object of worry.

The room was silent, her breathing the only sound, which in the silence seemed quite loud.

When you get that disease, you see, you lose your words.

It was over ten years ago that it first emerged, that mysterious disease with its unknown cause, but it was only about four years ago that it was officially named. Its proper name was something long and difficult, but if you put the first letters together it formed a word: SHED.

Tokino had found it so strange as she watched the initial press conference. Someone, maybe the Minister of Health, Labor, and Welfare or someone like that, was speaking solemnly, his face so serious, but it was weird to hear him spell it out—S-H-E-D— over and over, like it was a special surprise being kept from a child.

People began to talk about the disease using the contraction, saying someone had "begun shedding" in place of "became infected."

Like insects shedding their exoskeletons, people infected with the disease begin gradually losing their words. Eventually, they lose the ability to speak, to listen, to read, to write.

On the surface, these symptoms resembled aphasia or Alzheimer's disease, but there seemed to be no correspondence with psychological or neurological abnormalities, so it was difficult to address via speech therapy or traditional rehabilitation. In its final stages, not only communication but daily life itself became difficult for the afflicted. Some even became violent. People took to referring to those afflicted with SHED as "bugs."

Last autumn, a classmate of Tokino's granddaughter began shedding.

Her daughter has been anxious ever since.

She bought yards of organic cotton to make into masks, and their dinner table became crowded with mysterious fermented health foods, but even so, it seemed that it might just be a matter of time before they turned into bugs.

It seemed that people who lived in the same regions and places and in similar environments frequently started shedding within similar time frames.

At the same time, they said SHED wasn't contagious.

But mightn't it be like contagious menstruation, thought Tokino, *like how girls at the same school or living in the same dorm start to have periods that sync up?*

Tokino furrowed her brow, thinking about her granddaughter's classmate, whom she'd never met.

She's so young.

Tokino couldn't prevent the thought from arising.

If I could change places with her, I would.

Better that a useless old woman like me turn into a bug than a young person with hopes and dreams and a whole future ahead of her.

I mean, just look at me, this body I'm trapped in.

Even as she had these thoughts, though, Tokino couldn't help but shiver at the prospect of living out the rest of her years as a bug.

She said it aloud, softly.

"I want to die . . ."

The flowered mask muffled her voice. It sounded like someone else entirely.

The doorbell rang then, and she heard the sound of a woman's voice.

The homecare helper.

She'd been coming for months now, but Tokino could never remember her name, even though she'd heard it many times.

The woman was noisily entering the front door to the house.

Her bicycle key was attached to a key chain that had several good luck charms with bells on them, and they jingled and jangled with every step as she walked. The jingle-jangles got closer and closer until finally her face appeared at the door.

The woman's brown-dyed hair was held back with barrettes, a black polyurethane 3D-style mask covering her mouth. Though these days everyone wore masks.

It was like when radiation was falling from the sky, or when there was a contagious disease running rampant.

The onset of the disease could be slowed just by wearing a

mask, some said, or it would help slow the disease's progress. But people also seemed to wear them because they harbored the sneaking suspicion that the disease really was contagious after all. In any case, the medical reasons for wearing masks seemed rather muddled and unclear. They struck Tokino more as magic charms to keep words from spilling out and getting lost, or ritual boundaries to keep them safe and close.

Her flowered cotton mask still over her mouth, Tokino reluctantly turned her head toward the woman at the door and raised her voice as loud as she could to greet her.

"Thank you for coming all this way, even though you must be so busy."

It was such a bother how people seemed to assume that just because she'd lost the ability to move her body, she must also be on the verge of losing her words as well.

Having confirmed the presence of Tokino's voice, the woman entered the room.

The rented automatic bed was placed in a tatami-floored bedroom. This was where Tokino lay, but the woman entered the room without removing her slippers. *Don't you think you should take your slippers off to walk on the tatami?* thought Tokino, the words on the verge of leaving her mouth, but instead she just watched as the woman blithely did her chores without a second thought, clearing away the used tissues next to the automatic bed and throwing them in the wastebasket. The woman had over-plucked her eyebrows and failed to fill them back in, so all Tokino could look at was these hairless patches above her eyes.

In fact, everything this woman said or did disagreed with

Tokino; each and every little thing only irritated her more. She hated how she would stare at her phone, reading and writing messages the entire time she was here; she hated how she would fill out her daily reports on the dining room table without putting anything under them to protect the wood. The food she made was either over-seasoned or bland. And Tokino knew she brought food home with her all the time, pretending it was past its sell-by date and needed to be thrown away.

But what angered her most was knowing that if this woman wasn't here to look after her, she wouldn't be able to get along—the real object of her anger was herself.

It was humiliating.

I've got to calm down . . .

Whenever she felt like this, Tokino would seek solace in thinking about the great authors and poets in history.

For example, Virginia Woolf.

But what came to mind for her was not her great works like *Mrs. Dalloway* or *To the Lighthouse*; rather, Tokino would think about how she ended her life.

She walked into a river near her house and drowned.

She filled her pockets with stones to ensure her body would sink.

Coming back to herself after thinking this far, Tokino realized the woman was no longer in her room. She could hear the sound of water from the bathroom, where she was drawing a bath.

It was bath day, it seemed.

She spoke again, in a small voice.

"Ohh, I want to die . . . I want to die right now . . ."

Tokino recalled how, during the time she'd taken care of her father-in-law and then her husband, she'd had the thought, as she wiped shit from their dangling genitals, that she would never be able to tolerate that kind of humiliation herself.

Come to think of it, though, neither her husband nor his father had ever seemed particularly embarrassed by the situation. Was it that they'd spent their whole lives being taken care of, so they were used to it—that it just seemed natural to them that things would turn out this way? After all, well before they lost their faculties or became bedridden, Tokino had seen to their every bodily need already—their meals, their laundry, even their dirty underwear. It might not have seemed like any big deal to add wiping up their shit to the list.

But it wasn't like that for Tokino.

She'd been the one to care for others her whole life.

Being cared for by others was something she was completely unprepared to do.

⚶

White steam rose from the bath. It was a newfangled electric model that heated the water at the flip of a switch.

Tokino found herself lowered onto the rented pink plastic seat and then painstakingly undressed, layer by layer.

The bath played its little song signaling that the heating of the water was complete. It was "Dolly's Dreaming and Awakening," by Theodore Oesten.

Even the song made Tokino mad.

What would it mean for a dolly that can no longer move on its own, that can't even speak, to dream or wake up? Wouldn't it just mean more struggle, more pain?

The home care helper, still in her mask, had rolled up her sweatpants and stripped down to a black T-shirt before she'd started the process of removing Tokino's clothes: her flowered cotton mask; her maroon-striped pajamas, tops then bottoms; her beige chemise; and finally, her beige panties.

The woman was struggling, unable to slide the panties all the way off.

Tokino's slack, wrinkled stomach and thighs and the patches of shriveled pubic hair left on her half-bald genitals were completely exposed, but her soiled panties were caught on her cracked, powdery heels and weren't coming off.

She saw the scene in the mirror in all its laughable misery. It seemed like it was happening to someone else entirely.

Her immobile left leg hung heavily from the plastic seat.

Tokino recalled something from the diary Virginia Woolf left behind. She'd cited Henry James, writing:

> *Observe perpetually. Observe the income of age. Observe greed. Observe my own despondency. By that means it becomes serviceable. Or so I hope. I insist upon spending this time to the best advantage. I will go down with my colors flying. This I see verges on introspection; but doesn't quite fall in.*

This passage is from twenty days before her death.

Observe perpetually.

But when even observation proves useless, what's left to do?

Tokino breathed in through her nose and caught a whiff of fresh lemon scent. The woman must have cleaned. The lemon was the scent of the mildew-removing bathroom cleanser.

Finally, Tokino found herself guided the three steps it took to get her in the bath, where she was helped onto the shower stool. Looking down at the drain, she caught sight of an inchworm making its way along its edge.

She raised her voice again, softly.

"Ohh, I want to die . . ."

She felt the shower begin to pour down on her. Warm water flowed over her head and then over her whole body, wetting even the tips of her fingers and toes.

She watched as the water flowed into the bath to inundate the inchworm, bearing it along to disappear down the drain.

Tokino suddenly realized she had to urinate.

And then, just as suddenly, she realized she already was urinating, sitting there on the shower stool.

She watched the warm yellow liquid join the warm shower water flowing over her wrinkle-pleated thighs and then drain away.

3. CLASS

It was a new school year, and a new homeroom.

The first-year homeroom had been on the third floor, right next to the science classroom, but the second-year homeroom was on the second floor.

New homeroom, new classmates—Haru had the feeling that

everything should start anew, that this should be a brand-new start for a brand-new her. When something major happened in history, it signified a new era, a new period with a new name, but the reality was that even as everything seemed to change, it all actually remained the same. And so it was with this new school year—everything was exactly as the same as always.

Mrs. Tashiro was at the front of the class trying to demonstrate factorization, and Haru was sitting at her desk, her chin in her hands, a pale purple unwoven cotton mask over her mouth.

This pale purple mask was a product her mother had brought back from work, some special thing with amethyst somehow worked into it. *If you put this on, you won't start shedding, or if you do, it'll slow down the process*, she'd said. Haru couldn't help thinking that it seemed pretty unlikely that amethyst would make any difference one way or the other, and if it *were* true that wearing one would prevent shedding, surely everyone would be wearing one. But she wore it anyway, for her mother.

Last fall, her classmate Taguchi had started shedding.

People said that she was in a special institution now, for shedders.

Some called these special institutions *nests*. It seemed appropriate, conjuring images of bugs hibernating deep in the ground as if dead.

Though the institutions themselves used other words, describing themselves as nestled in "quiet areas, filled with green."

Haru typed the phrase into her phone.

Quiet areas, filled with green.

It seemed like the setup to a joke. After all, when you start shedding, first you lose your words, then your voice—"quiet areas" indeed.

Haru was writing as many jokes into her phone as she could. That way if she ever did start shedding she could have a sense of humor about it, at least at the beginning. Once she lost the ability to read, it all would be moot anyway.

Taguchi, the shedder, was the daughter of the owner of the convenience store facing the train station.

On her way back from her cram school one night just after New Year's, Haru passed the store and saw the front display window crisscrossed with masking tape, the words CURL UP AND DIE, PARASITE! spray-painted in big black letters across the wall next to it. It was terrible. She looked over at the electronic sign next to the parking lot and caught sight of a small swarm of ants gathered in the corner, even in the winter cold.

Mio-chan, who'd been good friends with Taguchi, had also seen the graffiti, and she seemed terribly depressed when Haru saw her at the cram school winter study session.

"It's so terrible what they wrote."

Haru and Mio-chan went to the same cram school and usually took the same train, but Mio-chan had fallen into a terrible depression since last fall.

That's when Taguchi'd started shedding, of course, but on top of that Mio-chan's grandmother, who lived in the house with her, had recently become bedridden after collapsing from an aneurysm or something. It seemed all she said these days was "I want to die," and Mio-chan said that now she might have to cut back her cram school sessions to just once a week.

One day on their way back from cram school, Haru and Mio-chan stopped by the family restaurant located on the bus terminal side of the train station. They ordered from the drink bar.

Haru, sucking her bright green melon soda through her straw, listened to what Mio-chan had to say.

"Taguchi's parents are having a really hard time."

Mio-chan was tearing up as she said this; she was wearing a flowered cotton mask that she pulled down slightly to take small sips from her mug of hibiscus tea.

"I can't believe there are people out there who'd do such a thing without a second thought."

Mio-chan wore her long black hair pulled back into a ponytail, various strands in the front pinned down with barrettes.

"I just can't believe it, that there would be people like that."

It hurt Haru's heart, too, to think of people calling Taguchi "bug" and "parasite" and telling her to "curl up and die." Haru nodded at Mio-chan's words, thinking about how cruel someone would have to be to break the windows and spray-paint terrible words on the walls of a store owned by people who'd more or less lost their daughter to illness.

Mio-chan set her white mug back on the table and spoke again.

"But even so, no matter what, I'm still happy she's alive, that I can be thankful she exists. I mean, every life has value, right? So just being alive—even if you're bedridden, or can't help anyone do anything, it's still a wonderful thing to be alive, right? It has meaning. I always think about that, about being glad someone hasn't died. But it seems that most people don't see that, they don't think that way, and that's what I find so hard to understand."

Haru sat still, watching the bubbles in her melon soda rise to the surface and then pop, shaken by Mio-chan's unflinching sincerity.

Mio-chan pulled her cotton mask back over her mouth, looked Haru straight in the eye, and said, "Haru, I have a favor to ask you."

She took Haru's hand in hers.

"In the event I achieve shedding, I want you—you in particular—to be happy for me, from the bottom of your heart. Please, can you do that?"

Haru was completely taken aback.

What are you saying, Mio-chan? You mean you actually want *to shed? You* want *to lose your words— to go from living as a person to living as a bug?*

Truth be told, Haru hadn't really known Taguchi all that well, and since she stopped coming to school shortly after she began shedding, she really didn't know what sort of state one falls into once it starts happening.

Thinking back, Haru recalled that at least on the outside, Taguchi gave a cheerful, plump impression with her big, dark eyes set against her pale skin, vaguely reminiscent of a silkworm's imago. She thought about Taguchi shedding, losing her words. Did she still look so happy now? Perhaps—happier than a worm boiled alive for its silk, at least.

Mio-chan was still looking straight at Haru.

"If you achieve shedding, Haru, I'll be happy for you, I promise."

Her eyes were depthlessly dark and clear.

Haru found herself nodding.

"I . . . I understand."

Mio-chan gripped Haru's hand harder and harder in hers. Her hand was cold and soft.

"I will, absolutely."

Her voice was muffled beneath her flowered cotton mask.

Haru nodded one more time.

Mio-chan is so kind.

Haru thought she understood why she continued to be so fastidious about wearing her mask: she cared so deeply about others that she couldn't bear to remove it. That seemed about right for someone as serious and scrupulous as her.

All at once, Mio-chan let go of Haru's hand and raised her mug of hibiscus tea to her mouth, quickly pulling her mask down just enough to take a sip before just as quickly pulling it back up.

Soon after this, Haru heard that one night, after a heavy snow had fallen on the town, Taguchi's father had had a heart attack and died. She saw her mother still at the register at the convenience store, though. She looked so tired, so old.

The next time Haru met Mio-chan was Friday night in the self-study classroom at the cram school.

Haru was sitting there drinking a carton of strawberry milk and eating a convenience store pastry in lieu of dinner when Mio-chan found her, rushing into the room in tears.

"Those shit people killed Taguchi's father! What a fucked-up world."

Haru was rather taken aback hearing Mio-chan use words like *shit people* and *fucked-up*.

"I'd rather turn into a bug than live as a piece of shit like them!

"We should give it all up, our words and everything else, just let it all go . . ."

Mio-chan murmured this last part to herself like a monologue beneath her flowered mask as she left Haru to go to her desk, where she took out a notebook and opened it up, revealing pages crammed with dense writing. Haru looked over at it from afar as she sucked strawberry milk through her straw.

I'd rather turn into a bug!

She remembered hearing that strawberry milk's pink color came from a dye made of crushed insects called cochineals. It still tasted just as sweet, though.

She'd only eaten half her pastry, but Haru quickly pulled her pale purple mask up from where it had slipped beneath her chin, re-covering her mouth. She knew there were people out there who thought SHED was a new stage of human evolution and that the afflicted were a select, elite group helping usher it in. She'd encountered believers in this theory on the way home from cram school, handing out pamphlets in front of the train station.

It was shocking to see the pamphleteers and speakers out in public, unmasked.

By giving up our words and achieving S-H-E-D, we can finally grow our true wings and fly!

All the terrible things happening in the world—war, disaster, disease—are the result of human arrogance, of trying to control light, even life itself—all that is properly God's domain!

Please join us in embracing the new world as it arrives!

The time for rebirth is now!

Haru would hurry by them holding her mask to her face with both hands, and she refused to take their pamphlets. They struck her as yet another new religion or self-help cult.

The speaker's words would drone on behind her until they were drowned out by the blaring sound of a passing advertising truck. Haru would hurry through the train station turnstiles without a second glance behind her.

Haru wondered these days if Mio-chan remembered the promise she'd made.

Such absolute promises were unreliable, she knew. When she'd been in middle school, she remembered making so many of them—that she would *absolutely* never have a boyfriend, that she would *absolutely* tell her friends if she lost her virginity—but all these unbreakable *absolutelys* ended up as so many *whatevers* in the end.

Mulling these things over, Haru looked back up at the blackboard.

The equations written there were all held together by parentheses.

Haru wondered how Taguchi was doing.

Like moths to a flame—the saying popped into Haru's head, like the memory of a prophecy.

🔥

It started with the news that a house where people were rumored to have begun shedding burned to the ground.

Four people were killed—the grandfather, the mother, the son, and the daughter. The father and the grandmother remained in critical condition.

The incident happened not even a year after the disease was named.

According to internet rumor, the grandmother and the father had been shedding in earnest, and the mother and son had also begun to lose their words. The grandfather and the daughter had yet to display symptoms, but the daughter had started to stay home from school. The daughter had talked with her friends on LINE about being afraid she might be starting to shed too.

In the end, it seemed that rather than go to the hospital, they chose to spread kerosene from their stove around the house and set it on fire; in other words, they chose death.

Like moths to a flame—or rather, like moths lighting a flame to fly into.

At least that's what people said on the internet.

Many were shaken by the incident at first. Before committing group suicide they should have gone to the hospital and sought medical help, they said.

The photos of their house that spread on the internet showed a contractor-built two-family home completely burned out, only the blackened walls remaining.

A middle-aged man, apparently a sociologist, held forth on the incident in a news site video, a knowing look on his face:

Of course, it's terrifying to face a disease that steals your words. But that's not the only factor behind this family's

suicide—there's also the desire not to trouble others, the
discrimination faced by those suffering from SHED, the
pressure to conform that excludes those who don't fit in.
Perhaps it is this traditional, oppressive society that needs to
be shed—not by them, but by us!

Sparks still glowed in the ruins of the fire-blackened house.

Perhaps the desire within bugs to fly into fire smolders the same way.

Perhaps when people begin to shed, they, like literal bugs, find themselves overcome by the desire to throw themselves into the blinding, burning light, even as they know it will destroy them.

People posted with increasing uneasiness and fear. All sorts of SHED-related opinions began to fly around, and a special SHED Information Hotline was set up.

But it didn't stop there.

Within a month following the family suicide, the special institutions for shedders began to go up in flames as well, one after another. A large number of casualties and even deaths resulted— not just SHED patients, but nurses and staff members as well.

Shedders' families began to appear on TV, bowing their heads and apologizing to the camera.

Hashtags like *#firebugs* and *#mothstoaflame* began to trend on Twitter.

And indeed, people began to say that shedders were not just *bugs* but also *firebugs*. Others floated the theory that it was staff who'd done it in an effort to exterminate the bugs. Some even tied the fires to the ancient Heian ritual of using rapeseed or whale oil to burn fields and drive out insects, delivering them to the world beyond.

In any case, the exact connection between shedding and fire remained unclear.

After all, most shedders couldn't leave a suicide note even if they wanted to, and those messages that were left behind on the internet or social media were basically unreadable.

And even for those who managed to escape death, most lost their words completely.

These poor souls were called *empty shells*.

An empty shell—as a person loses words one by one, soon their most distinguishing feature becomes their lack.

Their lack of words.

Tantamount to a lack of life, of existence.

As if to fill this lack, the phenomenon was debated to death, words piling up and repeating everywhere you looked.

I wonder what Mio-chan thinks about all this?

Haru looked over her shoulder out of reflex, but Mio-chan no longer sat behind her in this new school year; she was nowhere to be found.

Haru was scared of shedding.

She wrote her own name over and over in hiragana as if to fill in every inch of white space in her notebook. She assigned numerical values to each character, based on their vowels: *a* characters were 1, *i* characters 2, and so on. *Ha* was worth 1, *ru* 3. Haru's full family name, *ha* + *ru* + *ya* + *ma*, thus became 1311. She would then add up the pairs of numbers, then shift columns and do it again, finally producing a double digit result.

The result was 80.

This was the likelihood that Haru would start shedding.

She'd adapted this system from one she'd used in middle school using her name and the name of someone she liked to see how compatible they were.

Haru quickly crumpled up the sheet she'd used for her calculations and stuffed it in her pocket.

She knew several classmates had been using a Ouija board after school to figure out who would be the next to shed. They said that one time, they did it and the Sharpie everyone was holding had vibrated above the characters *ta* + *gu* + *chi*.

But what did it mean to name someone who'd already begun shedding?

Didn't it just prove that someone was surreptitiously moving the pen themselves?

After all, Haru was hardly the type to believe in things as flighty as fortunetelling or the spirit world.

Nevertheless, she found she couldn't stop doing it anyway. She was so anxious.

She wanted someone or something to tell her, *Don't worry, you're the exception, you'll never shed.* She wanted to feel reassured. Even if it was just a lie.

Likelihood to shed: 80 percent.

Eighty was also the atomic number of mercury. Haru recalled the periodic table that hung at the front of the science classroom. The numbers on it struck her now as a form of divination.

She'd read somewhere on the internet that people were swallowing mercury to prevent shedding.

There were even rumors that some of her classmates had broken open old thermometers they'd found and drunk the mercury. The prices of vintage thermometers had apparently skyrocketed on websites like eBay and Mercari.

Haru hid her phone beneath her textbook and began researching it.

She found an article talking about the Qin Emperor, the first Emperor of China, who drank mystical elixirs of mercury because he believed they would make him immortal. As part of his bid for eternal life, he built an enormous tomb that featured a hundred rivers of mercury. Of course, in the end, it was the mercury he drank that significantly shortened his life.

Haru bookmarked the page on her phone.

Good material for a joke, she thought.

What period am I living in, again? Haru adjusted her pale purple mask, but she found she couldn't bring herself to laugh at it.

Committing suicide became glorified on the internet, referred to as "shattering like a jewel."

A popular male comedian rumored to have started shedding had left a message on Twitter and then committed suicide: *Rather than live on and bring shame upon my name, I choose to fall in glory.* The internet was quick to compare this to "shattering like a jewel," and thus a meme was born.

The comedian had written his note before he'd lost his words completely, hanging himself in his apartment. *I guess it beats turning into a bug, starting a fire, and then dying anyway,* thought Haru, but she found she couldn't laugh at this either.

About a month before shattering like a jewel, the comedian's social media accounts had been plagued with trolls saying things like, *I heard this guy was funny but lately he hasn't made me laugh once—is this because of shedding?* or *I'm afraid to go to his live shows, he might light the place on fire!* There were messages that went further, saying, *Die already, bug!* and *Why are we using tax money to keep dangerous bugs like this alive?* The news reported that his people were worried he'd taken these comments to heart.

Haru read a tweet left by a fan of his who seemed to be in middle school.

I can't believe he's dead. At least the words he left behind will live forever. RIP.

Many found the "shatter like a jewel" phrase problematic due to its previous use to glorify mass and forced suicides during World War II. Others objected not due to glorifying suicide but rather because it cheapened the memory of the wartime heroes the term evoked, while yet others pointed out that the term had been also been used to refer to confessing one's love only to be rejected: the debate over the meaning and correctness of words raged on and on.

As it did, some started to make a point of praising those who'd "shattered like jewels," and it became a bit of a trend.

Thank you for doing us the favor of dying.

They would leave this as a comment on posts by families of those who'd committed such a suicide.

Haru had it written in her phone, too.

Thank you for doing us the favor of dying.

It sounded like the kind of thing you'd say after someone

came in and Marie-Kondoed a room for you, throwing away a bunch of useless stuff—not bad joke material.

Haru found herself seriously contemplating sneaking into the science classroom to drink mercury.

4. MENSTRUAL CYCLE

Mitsuko sat alone on the school toilet, staring at two pink lines.

The lines in the little window on the pregnancy test in her hand stood out so crisply, undeniably. They meant that Mitsuko's body held a new life somewhere within it.

She couldn't help but be shaken by the emotion swelling within her.

It was an emotion stirred by the sheer prospect of humans continuing to create life by their own hand even as so many, by their own hand, were extinguishing it.

As Marie Curie had said about laboratories when she managed to create her own—the Radium Institute—quoting the great nineteenth-century biochemist Louis Pasteur:

> *They are the temples of the future, wealth, and well-being.*
> *It is here that humanity will grow, strengthen, and*
> *improve . . . humanity's own works are all too often those of*
> *barbarism, fanaticism, and destruction.*

A day will come, surely, when the present disease will be eradicated as well.

Just as so many fearsome contagious and genetic diseases

have been conquered, one day SHED too will be a thing of the past.

Everything presently shrouded in ignorance will come to light eventually, and the day may come when immortality itself may be a reality.

These were the thoughts Mitsuko had, sitting there with her panties around her ankles.

It suddenly came to her that she should send her sister a LINE message telling her of her good news.

She fished her phone out of the pocket of the skirt still pooled around her feet.

She opened LINE and saw that her last message was still unread.

This bothered her a little, but she decided to send a message anyway.

She tapped the screen.

The little keyboard appeared.

But her finger didn't move.

The cursor sat there, blinking.

For some reason, the words just didn't come.

Mitsuko froze where she sat, one hand holding this plastic object with its two pink lines, the other holding her phone.

This can't be true . . .

It's just a moment of forgetfulness, she told herself.

Nonetheless, she was gripped with unease.

As SHED advances, people usually lose between one hundred and two hundred words a day—up to five hundred sometimes, depending on the case. There's seemingly no rhyme or reason to which words disappear first—whether they're words used only seldomly or words used frequently in everyday life—and some of the afflicted even fail to notice for a while that it's happening at all.

Whatever the case, though, she had to calm down.

Mistuko concentrated on thinking about Marie and Pierre Curie again. About Marie placing "my child, radium," next to her pillow as it glowed with pale blue fairy light. About Pierre performing an experiment in which he pressed "my child, radium" against his arm until it left a burn.

Mitsuko was able to formulate these thoughts in her head as words without any seeming trouble. She regained a bit of her composure.

The Curies discovered that radium's radioactivity killed cells. This meant that it would kill cancerous cells as well, which meant it had the potential to cure cancer.

The Curies, and in fact the whole world, had such high hopes.

This new element could be the miracle cure humanity has been waiting for!

The day may be near when cancer itself will be eradicated!

One person who shared these hopes was the wealthy American industrialist Joseph M. Flannery.

His younger sister—or was it his elder?—was suffering from cancer at the time.

Joseph wanted to get his hands on radium to use as medicine for his sister. But radium was so very expensive at the time that even with his riches, he was unable to acquire any.

He was disappointed, but he did not give up. He would do anything to save his sister's life. He wanted to save any life that could be saved—no one, whether rich or poor, should ever die of cancer again.

And he knew he had the resources to make this a reality.

So he created the Standard Chemical Company—a factory for refining radium. It was the site of the world's first commercial production of radium.

Low-cost radium was suddenly plentiful. Though by the time this became a reality, his sister had already passed away.

Radium water, radium oil, radium paint.

Joseph was convinced that radium could cure a variety of afflictions, not just cancer, and lauded its efficacy far and wide in treating "mental disease, tuberculosis, rheumatism, even anemia."

Marie Curie made a point of visiting his facility during her tour of America. But Joseph never realized his dream of meeting her.

For he had already succumbed to radiation poisoning and died.

Mitsuko reached this point in her train of thought and shuddered.

Well, I might as well pull my pants up.

The toilet was filled with yellow liquid. She had the nagging feeling this should be meaningful to her, but she couldn't place why.

The Curies were plagued by mysterious illnesses. Pierre suffered from rheumatism, while Marie chronically sleepwalked. But what made Marie suffer most was her miscarriage. It had apparently been a daughter she lost.

Mitsuko could no longer find the small fly that had been sitting on the sanitary napkin disposal box. She left the bathroom stall without even flushing the toilet.

This morning, too, she'd seen a shedder's family apologizing on TV.

We are so very sorry for all the trouble we've caused.

Mitsuko looked at herself in the mirror at the sink, then turned the silver knob on the faucet.

Clear water rushed out in a flood.

H_2O.

Two atoms of oxygen and one of hydrogen.

She put a finger into the stream. It felt cold.

She tried to grasp the water.

Water was H_2O.

It passed between her fingers and drained away.

It disappeared.

She'd heard that deaf people had started to be mistaken for shedders and assaulted.

She'd heard that some people had been misdiagnosed with SHED and killed themselves, and their families were now suing the doctors. They had only lost their voice due to a cough, it turned out.

She heard a firetruck's siren blare somewhere, then fade away. Another fire.

She'd heard there were babies born these days who never cried.

But, wait. She'd just learned something. Something that made her happy. She couldn't put her finger on what it had been, though. What was it?

Mitsuko looked down at the object still gripped tightly in her hand. She stared at it.

The two lines in the little window meant something important, she could feel it.

It looked like some sort of laboratory tool, used in experiments.

Out in the hall, the window was filled with the pale light of evening.

Everywhere around her was silent.

Then, from far away, she heard a tiny sound.

Oh that's right, I need to lock up.

Mitsuko supposed the ant she'd seen writhing in corner of the stairwell must be long dead by now.

She took a step.

Her jade-green spring coat fluttered around her, as if shivering.

Harry's heart liebt Berlin butterflies!

H for hydrogen. He for helium. Li for lithium. Be for beryllium. B for boron.

Liebt *means* loves *in German.*

C for carbon. N for nitrogen. O for oxygen. F for fluorine. Ne for neon.

Mitsuko ascended the stairs.

With every step, Mitsuko hummed along with the mnemonic she used to name all the elements on the periodic table in order.

That table invented in the nineteenth century by the Russian chemist Dmitri Mendeleev.

It allowed us to see how every single thing in the world was based on cycles, on set periods. Such a vital step in the march of knowledge, Mitsuko thought.

A menstrual cycle was a period of 28 days.

A lunar cycle was a period of 29.5 days.

The Earth's journey around the sun was a period of 365 days.

And so, humans came to know the moon, came to know the sun.

They came to understand the passage of months, of years, of seasons.

Cells live for a time, then die. As do eggs.

As do people. As do insects.

But at the time the periodic table was created, there were still various blanks left to be filled in. For example Ga, for gallium. Or Ge, for germanium.

There were spots left open even now for elements yet to be discovered.

After all, at the time the periodic table was created, no one suspected the existence of electrons or neutrons.

No one suspected that atoms—a term invented to name the smallest indivisible particles imaginable—would one day be split.

But scientists carry on discovering new elements one after another.

They give them names, and with these new names, they're able to hold them in their hands.

They're able to fill in the blanks, one by one.

The atomic number of radium, the element discovered and named by the Curies, is 88.

The element polonium, named for Marie's home country of Poland, is 84.

Mitsuko continued humming her song

... *Sips* ... *what did that stand for again?*

It's Na for natrium, Mg for magnesium, Al for aluminum. So sips *would be Si for silicon, P for Phosphorous, and then S for . . . for . . .*

Mitsuko stopped humming.

Blanks were opening up all over her periodic table.

All the things she'd held in her hands, that she should be able to hold in her hands, were slipping her grasp one by one and disappearing.

Like the exoskeletons shed by insects as they grow, one after another after another . . .

She was shedding.

Mitsuko reached the second-floor landing and then stopped, just for a moment.

5. ENDPOINT

After being lifted from the bath, Tokino found herself placed, stark naked, back on the plastic chair facing the sink.

Steam had risen from the hot water and clouded the mirror with white fog.

The woman silently wiped Tokino's body dry, rubbed it with lotion, and then methodically dressed it in new clothes, one layer at a time: brand new white panties, then yellow pajamas that were patterned, top and bottom, with blue polka dots.

Tokino sat in the chair and allowed her unresponsive arms and legs to be manipulated however the woman wished.

The last thing to be put on was the flowered cotton mask across her mouth.

Tokino found herself getting mad again.

It wasn't because it was irritating to have a mask crammed on her face, though it was.

It was because she'd noticed that the lavender-scented candle that was supposed to be next to the mirror had disappeared, along with its holder.

Had her daughter thrown it out?

Had she really gone so far as to throw out a *scented candle*?

It's true that ever since her daughter had seen on the news that shedders seemed to be starting fires, she'd been obsessed with fire safety around the house. She'd thrown away everything, not just lighters and matches but even the benzine they'd bought as stain cleaner.

When her daughter had moved in after her divorce, she'd converted the bath to this electric model. She'd planned to convert the kitchen to induction heat as well, but the installation costs were higher than she'd bargained for and the gas stove had remained. But now she regretted it, lamenting that it should have been converted to induction even if she'd have had to go into debt to do it. She'd applied to have it done now, but it would be a half-year wait.

Her daughter frowned in despair as she affixed however many handmade flowered cotton masks to her face every day. She made a point of forbidding Tokino from using the gas range.

"Ohh, I want to die . . ."

Perhaps she didn't hear her, or perhaps it was just out of sheer pique, but the woman never acknowledged it when Tokino said this.

Tokino could see that the bald patches where she'd over-plucked her eyebrows were beaded in sweat. They looked like clusters of tiny insects.

Tokino consoled herself by thinking once more of Virginia Woolf.

She'd killed herself while the war had still been raging.

It might not be so rare for someone surrounded by great numbers of people dying, who didn't know if or when she might die as well, to choose to take her own life.

The air raids had begun in London. She still published books and continued her work, but she had to evacuate London for Lewes. Even in this evacuation zone, though, bombs still fell nearby; two had fallen by the river and remained there, unexploded, marked by white wooden crosses.

In the face of this, Virginia writes:

I said to L: I don't want to die yet.

Soon after, she imagines a bomb falling directly on her—she imagines her own death:

I've got it fairly vivid—the sensation: but can't see anything but suffocating nonentity following after. I shall think—oh I wanted another 10 years—not this—and shan't, for once, be able to describe it. It—I mean death.

It was only six months before her suicide that she wrote this. Is that what she really thought, at the end, sinking to the bottom of the river?

—oh I wanted another 10 years—

Supported by the woman gripping her by the shoulder and around her hips, Tokino walked toward her bed.

One step, then another.

Her legs buckled from time to time, and she nearly fell.

Tokino had lived almost twenty years longer than Virginia had. Yet, would she think the same when death finally approached?

—oh I wanted another 10 years—

By the time she managed make it to the edge of the bed and sit down, then turn her body so she could lie back down again, beads of sweat had started to pop out on her own forehead. Her flowered cotton mask stuck to her sweat-slicked cheeks and nose.

The clock on the wall read six o'clock.

Her daughter would be coming home soon.

Tokino peeled off her mask and brought her mug to her mouth, sipping the thickener-laced hot water it held. Then she put on her reading glasses and awkwardly opened the newspaper to wait for her daughter's return.

The first article her eyes landed on was about how in China, not only humans but also six police dogs had begun shedding. On top of that, the afflicted dogs happened to be clones.

Tokino hadn't even realized there were already in the world such things as cloned dogs; she felt like she was reading about the future.

According to the article, the six dogs had been cloned from

the skin cells of a highly trained canine agent; they were Kunming wolfdogs, apparently. A color photo accompanied the article, showing the black-nosed, tawny-coated dogs with their handlers standing on a tiered stage somewhere. Probably a press conference announcing their induction into the police force. The Chinese government was reportedly instituting policies to swiftly curb the disease's spread, as well as making plans to re-clone more dogs from the original skin cells, which had been kept in storage.

Tokino ran her right hand across the close-clipped hair covering her scalp.

Her hair, once long enough to weave into a braid, had been shaven during her hospitalization after her cerebral hemorrhage.

The sun visible through her window was setting.

The article didn't say what happened to the police dogs who'd begun shedding, but she figured they must have been put to sleep. It didn't seem logical that police dogs that were no longer of any use would be allowed to live.

After all, even leftover dogs and cats in pet shops ended up sent to pounds and eventually destroyed.

In other words, it took money and effort to sustain life, and also to end it.

A few days ago, a politician got into deep trouble for a joke he made during a speech, saying that if only we could send shedders to the gas chamber, the tax money used to support them could be freed up to be spent on other things.

A special news program on the issue was aired, showing interviews with people protesting his words.

Does he think if all the shedders just did us the favor of dying, everything would be better? Is that what "personal responsibility" means now?

Tokino noticed a tiny black speck on the duvet.

Thinking it was an insect, she used the edge of the newspaper to lift it off the bed, only to realize it was just a piece of lint.

She had to laugh.

An old woman like me, useless, unable to help anyone do anything— how am I any different than a bug?

Come to think of it, though, I guess I'm even lower than a bug.

A bug can "shatter like a jewel" and everyone will thank them for doing them the favor of dying.

Tokino found herself unable to stop laughing.

"Ah—aha—ahahaha—"

The thickened water she'd swallowed threatened to come back up, and she forced it back down so she wouldn't vomit.

After all, when did I ever have words of my own to express? Was there ever a time when tried to make anyone listen to me, even once?

"Aha—haha—ahahahaha . . ."

Finally, silence returned to the room.

It was so quiet.

Too quiet.

Tokino listened to the sound of chopping from the kitchen, then listened to it stop.

The woman was preparing dinner, it seemed, but it was strange. Usually, she would bother Tokino with incessant questions about what she wanted, where spices were kept, etcetera, etcetera. She realized that today, though, she hadn't heard the woman's voice even once.

Could it be—?

Thinking back, she remembered that her daughter had been angry with her too, saying that her daily report hadn't been filled out properly.

Tokino's breath caught in her throat.

Was that woman losing her words?

Was she beginning to shed?

Was she becoming a bug?

All of a sudden, this disease that had seemed so distant, something only read about in the newspaper or seen on TV, became something close—too close. It was true that her granddaughter's classmate had come down with it, too, but she'd never even seen that girl's face.

Would the woman choose to shatter like a jewel?

Tokino looked over at the bay window from her bed and caught sight of a praying mantis, its pale green wings open wide. Taking her reading glasses off, she peered at the mantis and saw it was dead, carried along by three little ants.

The ants were so small, but they were able to support the weight of the mantis that was so many times bigger than they were, pulling it along, moving it around. The mantis's pale green wings would, from time to time, jostle and come loose from the body, spreading wide as if in flight.

Tokino watched its progress for a while.

Then she took the edge of the newspaper and flicked it to the ground.

It's quite a phrase they use, "shatter like a jewel."

Mothers throwing their children off cliffs, then jumping after them to their deaths. Soldiers testifying to how they found babies hidden in caves and ran them through with their swords. The arms and legs of those unable to accept surrender, blown apart after pulling the pin of an unexploded hand grenade.

Tokino was born the autumn of the year Japan lost the war, so for her "shattering like a jewel" was the stuff of newspapers and black-and-white movies. But she remembered a middle-aged lady she'd seen once at someone's funeral—she couldn't recall whose—while she was still a little girl.

Michi-chan, her cousin, had told her.

That woman there, you see her? She killed her child by her own hand!

Tokino remembered the phrase so clearly.

By her own hand!

The woman's right hand had a dull gold ring on one finger and a web of bumpy veins across its back.

Young Tokino couldn't take her eyes off it.

She watched as the woman used it to grip a knife and peel an apple. She watched as she used it to pick up a bottle of beer and pour some into a glass.

How did she use that hand when she killed her child?

Did she close it around the child's throat? Did she use it to press silk wadding against its mouth? Did she use it to raise the child up and then smash it against the ground?

She couldn't stop looking, or imagining.

Suddenly, young Tokino realized she'd wet herself. Warm liquid ran down her thighs to her feet. Her nice socks with their white ribbons were stuck to her toes, soaked.

The woman picked up a nearby cloth napkin with her hand, then ran over and used it to assiduously wipe up Tokino's urine as it spread across the wood floor.

Decades had passed since then.

That woman was surely dead by now.

Tokino threw the newspaper down onto the bed and replaced the flowered cotton mask on her face. Her breath seeped from the mask and fogged up her reading glasses, turning the world beyond them a cloudy white.

She parted her lips.

And then let out a scream.

It was directed at the woman.

"Oh! I want to die!"

She screamed again, this time at the top of her lungs.

"Oh! I want to die! Right now!"

Silence.

The woman made no reply.

The silence seemed to last for an eternity.

In lieu of a reply, white smoke began to seep up from the kitchen.

Smoke!

And some sort of horrible smell.

Typical.

Burning out the bottom of the pot.

Nonetheless, Tokino's heartbeat quickened.

She needed to calm down.

She tried to think of Virginia Woolf. But all that came to mind was her suicide note.

I can't fight any longer. I know that I am spoiling your life, that without me you could work. And you will I know. You see, I can't even write this properly. I can't read. What I want to say is I owe all the happiness in my life to you.

It occurred to Tokino that Virginia may have been shedding. She may have been scared of becoming a bug.

The note she wrote sounds, after all, just like the notes left behind by those who go on to shatter like jewels.

Tokino began to cough, spasms that mixed with rising laughter.

"Ahh—ahhh ahhh—ahahaha—ahahaha—"

But what if the one reading was actually you, and the one writing actually me?

Would I agree that you had "spoiled my life"?

I might.

If you hadn't been there, would I have been able to work?

I might.

I would probably have been able to work.

I certainly might have actually worked.

But you are not me.

And you could never understand whether my life was "spoiled" or not.

My work was something I did—me! It was never something that depended on you.

"Ahh—ahhh ahhh—ahahaha—ahahaha—"

It was getting brighter and brighter, out beyond the white smoke.

Tokino wanted to deliver her words to the woman. But she was surely gone by now, dead.

"Ahhh—hahaaa—hhhhhh—"

Brightness was all around, surrounding her with blinding light.

The flames seemed to dance, back and forth and back and forth.

"Haha—haha—

"Haaaa—hhhhhaaa—"

Had the woman heard me, though?

Had the woman heard the words I screamed?

Tokino suddenly grew agitated, trying to raise her left hand to wipe the fog from her reading glasses with her sleeve. But of course her hand could no longer grasp a thing.

Ahhh . . .

Ahhh . . .

She heard the sound of the front door opening.

6. ERA

Classes were over, but Haru remained in the classroom, alone.

She watched through the window as lights blinked on in the apartment buildings outside and airplanes drew white lines across the pale evening sky. A column of mosquitos rose from the biotope in the schoolyard.

It was hard to believe that this was a place where so many people were falling ill and dying. It would have felt more appropriate if she'd looked out and seen ruined buildings surrounded by piles of bricks and burned-out remnants where houses once stood. Or even just abandoned streets, workers clad in protective hazmat suits the only living things left.

But what she saw instead was a normal, everyday street lined with convenience stores and supermarkets.

A woman pushing a baby carriage.

A man with a square black delivery bag strapped to his back, riding a bicycle.

Children walking down the sidewalk wearing matching backpacks branded with the logo of their cram school.

Looking down at the scene, everything bad seemed like it must be happening in another world, far away from here.

Haru drew in a deep breath beneath her ill-fitting pale purple mask.

It tasted stale, humid.

She slung her navy-blue bag over her shoulder and prepared to leave the classroom. Her bag was covered with patches, but the cloth was starting to wear through in places, leaving holes that made it look moth-eaten.

She took a step.

On second thought, sneaking into the science classroom to swallow mercury was too much, even as a joke.

But what was there left for her to do?

Just sit quietly and wait to start shedding?

Just wait, shivering in her pale purple mask?

Haru recalled a girl who'd gotten famous by shedding.

The girl was a YouTuber, and she was showered in attention after broadcasting her SHED diagnosis and then starting a thirty-day countdown to when she planned to shatter like a jewel. Haru remembered her huge, dark pupils, how they'd reminded her of a dragonfly's compound eyes.

Many reacted with sympathy, leaving messages begging her not to die and sending her chains of paper cranes. Many others simply watched as she maintained her silence.

It was a silence that, if it were happening on TV, would seem like a broadcast interruption.

After she received so much attention, shedders of all kinds began to appear in social media: shedding musicians, shedding internet entrepreneurs, shedding fashion models . . . but they all ended up ignored or, even if they managed to attract some attention at first, rapidly fading away. People said that losing your popularity was an even quicker death than losing your words. People began calling such ephemeral shedding celebrities mayflies.

Even the YouTuber girl was a mayfly of sorts, and her popularity didn't last in the end. The date of her scheduled shattering came and went and yet she didn't die, disappointing and then eventually irritating her fans.

What a faker!

She might be a pretty YouTuber but she's still just a stupid bug.

How disgusting, using SHED for attention!

She eventually had to hire security to protect the apartment where she lived alone, out of fear of her most fervent fans and the threats of violence she was receiving.

At long last, after receiving nothing but criticism and jeers, her broadcast abruptly stopped.

According to internet rumor, her parents, who lived somewhere out in the country, finally committed her to a nest. Perhaps you could say she'd become a true "underground idol" at last.

In any case, by then she had likely lost most of her words anyway, so you could also say she was fortunate, as any hurtful comments that came her way could no longer do her any harm.

Haru had all this written down in her phone. Plenty of good joke material, after all.

It was so quiet.

All the students must be gone by now, and most of the teachers must surely be in their lounge.

Haru left the classroom and ascended the staircase.

One step, then another . . .

She reached the landing and stopped.

She thought she heard a sound.

She looked up and caught sight of a spider crawling across the ceiling.

Haru was seized briefly by the impulse to turn heel and run away, but soon got a grip on herself. She remembered that the science classroom was supposed to be cursed. People blamed the curse for Miss Mitsuko's two miscarriages and her apparent inability to have a baby. So girls who wanted to lose their unwanted pregnancies had taken to sneaking into the science classroom lately to take advantage of the curse's effects.

So if it were Miss Mitsuko in there, she would just wonder why Haru was still hanging around and leave it at that, and if it were another student, they'd just become accomplices in sneaking around.

No one would actually suspect that she'd been sneaking in to swallow mercury.

Step by step, Haru drew closer.

After all, what on earth did Miss Mitsuko think she was doing, anyway?

Haru thought this as she pulled her pale purple mask, which had slipped down under her chin, back up over her mouth.

She couldn't imagine wanting to bring a child into this world on purpose.

🔥

Just as she suspected, the sound was coming from inside the science classroom.

The door was open.

Haru caught sight of yet another little spider, this one crawling through the gap between the door and the wall.

She slowly poked her head into the classroom, both hands holding her mask to her face.

She saw rows of empty seats.

She saw chalk dust on the desk in front of the blackboard.

She turned her head toward the window and saw it was wide open.

Gray curtains fluttered in the breeze.

She saw a shadow in the shape of a person standing before it.

A student.

Her reddish-brown skirt was hiked up around her waist.

What year was she?

Her long black hair was pulled back into a single ponytail, which bounced up and down.

One foot was up on the windowsill.

Was she preparing to jump?

Only a few days before, a student had jumped out a window at the cram school in an attempt to shatter like a jewel. It was a third-year student who'd always been in the highest percentile when they took the nationwide mock exams, but her grades had taken a sudden downturn, at which point she realized she was shedding. Her older sister and younger brother had previously shed, and these hard experiences had made her want to go to medical school and become a SHED researcher working to develop treatments for it. In the end, she jumped but she didn't die, only breaking some bones. Still, her parents held the cram school liable and took them to court.

That girl would never try to "shatter like a jewel" or anything like that!

It must have been an accident.

Ever since, the cram school windows have been double-locked.

The least she could have done was do us the favor of dying properly—look at the mess she's made! Haru remembered hearing her fellow students talking like this in the cram school classroom.

With the windows like this, if one of us started to shed, we'd all be locked in as the place burned to the ground!

Haru remembered looking at the newly double-locked windows. Everyone says it so easily, *Do us the favor of dying*. But when it really happens they can't handle being involved. It's as if what people really want is for bugs to crawl somewhere out of sight to die.

But right now, the science classroom window was wide open right in front of her.

Gray curtains were fluttering in the breeze.

Haru didn't know if she should stop this jewel from shattering too.

But before she knew it, she was running toward the window.

Her foot still on the windowsill, the student turned slowly to look at her.

Haru cried out without thinking.

"Mio-chan!"

It was Mio-chan.

Mio-chan as she always was, the stray hairs above her forehead fastidiously pinned down, a flowered cotton mask carefully affixed to her face.

Mio-chan's body jerked with surprise.

Her pale thighs shone in the light, exposed beneath her hiked-up skirt.

The two girls looked directly in each other's eyes.

Mio-chan was silent.

Silent.

Haru wondered if Mio-chan had already lost her words.

But you wanted so badly to shed!

You said that if you achieved shedding, you wanted me—me in particular—to be happy for you.

Happy for you, from the bottom of my heart.

You held my hand.

You promised.

Absolutely.

And now here you are, trying to shatter like a jewel!

Haru felt something akin to betrayal.

But then Mio-chan nervously pulled her mask down, exposing her mouth, and slowly parted her lips.

"I don't think I can shed, Haru."

Her voice sounded clear as always, not muffled or blurry at all. Mio-chan still had her words.

Haru could see a little white tooth peeking out from behind her dainty lips.

Shocked at her words, Haru couldn't think of what to say.

Wha—?

Mio-chan was the soul of sincerity. Her lips parted again.

"So I decided to try reincarnation."

And then she smiled a little. Haru noticed for the first time that she was slightly bucktoothed.

Mio-chan was still looking straight at Haru.

"According to Buddhist teachings, when you do bad things you end up reborn in the realm of bugs and beasts, right? Maybe this way, I can become a real bug."

Her eyes were so dark and clear.

What is she talking about?

Haru was at a loss for words.

Mio-chan seemed to sincerely believe that since she couldn't seem to become a bug by shedding, she would try to become a literal insect.

Mio-chan continued to speak confidently, her mask still hooked under her chin.

"Being a bug seems much more respectable than being a piece-of-shit human anyway."

And with that, Mio-chan turned back toward the open window and went about finishing her preparations for jumping.

She stood up in the window, spreading her arms wide like wings.

She lifted a foot.

And then it happened—the door to the science classroom slammed shut with a bang.

The two girls turned to look at it.

Miss Mitsuko, her hand still pressed against the door, was looking in their direction, her eyes wide. She began to walk straight toward them without saying a word.

Her jade-green spring coat swirled around her like the still-wet wings of a cicada newly emerged from the ground.

The two girls stared at Miss Mitsuko as she approached.

Silence.

Miss Mitsuko wasn't saying a word.

She just silently walked toward them.

It seemed possible she might even encourage Mio-chan to shatter like a jewel.

Haru waited for her to speak.

Miss Mitsuko walked right up to Haru and Mio-chan and stopped. Still, she kept her silence behind her white unwoven mask.

Haru and Mio-chan remained silent as well.

It was a long silence.

Miss Mitsuko then extended her right hand and wordlessly showed them the object it held.

Filled with trepidation, the two girls hesitantly peered into her hand.

It looked like a small thermometer.

No, not a thermometer.

A pregnancy test.

Not only that, they could clearly see two pink lines in the little window.

One foot still on the windowsill, Mio-chan turned to look at Haru, who returned her gaze from where she stood rooted to the floor beside the window.

The result was positive.

In other words, she was pregnant.

Haru was once again at a loss for words.

What is going on?

She slowly looked back at Miss Mitsuko.

But she still just stood there, silent.

She seemed to be making no effort to say a word.

Haru had no idea what she was trying to communicate with this pantomime.

And then it came to her: perhaps Miss Mitsuko thought she and Mio-chan had snuck into the science classroom because they wanted to abort an unwanted pregnancy. And so she thought she'd display this before their eyes. To demonstrate that curses didn't exist—not in this classroom, not anywhere.

She would fulfill her mission as a teacher of science.

If so, what a wild misunderstanding!

Haru couldn't help but stifle a laugh.

Though, come to think of it, maybe it wasn't as far off the mark as it seemed.

Both Haru and Mio-chan had come to this room to rid themselves of something.

Something unwanted, like an unwelcome baby.

Or a wished-for baby who never arrived.

A thin thread of spider's silk hung from the ceiling in the corner of the room.

Hanging there, so very thin, it glittered faintly in the light as it moved in the breeze.

But still, what a moment to tell us about her pregnancy!

Haru made a mental note to be sure to write all this down in her phone.

But wait—why was she making these notes again, exactly?

Haru stood there, silent behind her pale purple mask.

Mio-chan spoke, her voice soft, her foot still on the windowsill.

"Congratulations."

Haru's reddish-brown skirt moved softly in the breeze, like slowly unfurling wings.

THE FLYING
TOBITA SISTERS

THE GLASS IN the windows of the buildings spread out before me glittered like so many scattered jewels. The city lay at my feet. I could see the roofs of individual houses and modest apartment buildings in the valleys dividing the high rises, and between them, trees sprouted fresh new growth, glimpses of green like stitches in the urban fabric. A broad strip of asphalt ran perfectly straight through it, crossing the city's center on its way to the sea.

I took a deep breath. It tasted of spring. And then, following the path of the road below me toward the sea, I flew. My hair,

my tie, the cord of the earphones pumping music into my ears—
all fluttered in the wind as I took off. There were some strong winds
up here. On the verge of losing my balance, I used my wings like
a rudder to right myself.

As I was doing so, my wings flapping as I twisted in the air,
my bag, which was hanging at an angle from my body, came
dangerously close to snagging on a lightning rod extending up
from one of the high-rise roofs.

The wind in spring was dangerous, not only because of its un-
predictable gustiness, but also because of the yellow dust it gathered as it swirled and eddied across the ground. The air around me
was foggy with pollen and dust, and I blinked again and again to
clear the particles from my eyes.

Looking behind me, I could see my classmate Makino bob-
bing around in the air behind me, buffeted too by the wind. He
was clutching his overstuffed bookbag to his side, his gold-rimmed
glasses ready to fly right off his face. This would be a day when it
would be better to fly low than high, it seemed.

Our ancestors had tried for centuries to fly.

Icarus tried it using bird feathers fixed with wax; Leonardo
da Vinci left behind detailed, scientifically-sound drawings of
possible flying machines; the legendary Chinese military strate-
gist Zhuge Liang may or may not have invented the hot air bal-
loon; Abbas ibn Firnas attempted to fly off a cliff in Cordoba only
to fall to the earth, injuring himself. In Japan, the inventor Chūha-

chi Ninomiya designed flying machines whose mechanisms imitated crows and jewel beetles, but he ended up abandoning them after he failed to get his hands on the right engine—there are so many tales and legends like this left from the world before flight.

My mother had worked as a researcher at a university and devoted herself to the study of such attempts. She focused her studies especially on Otto Lilienthal. Born in nineteenth-century Prussia, Otto and his brother Gustav studied the mechanics of bird flight, eventually developing contraptions that would allow humans to do the same. They concentrated especially on the wings of storks and cranes, and finally constructed an artificial cone-shaped "flying hill" near Berlin that was fifteen meters high; Otto jumped from it over and over, fitted with wings modeled on the birds he studied.

My mother had one of Lilienthal's bird sketches pinned to the wall near her bed. She would show me pictures of the wings and gliders he designed that allowed him to fly. Of course, in the end, he fell to the earth during one of his flights and died.

Our ancestors wanted so badly to fly into the air. I want to understand how they felt, looking up at the sky but unable to fly . . .

My mother fluffed up her hair and wings as she said this, her eyes shining. I was still in elementary school then, and she was talking about this with me and my father as he fluttered around the kitchen making dinner. He was frying fish on the range, steam rising in white clouds from the pan. Felix, our tortoiseshell cat, was napping under the table, and my mother reached down to give him a pet as she continued to talk, her wings quivering with excitement.

The Wright brothers, hearing of Lilienthal's death, redoubled their efforts to make their own flying machine, and in 1903, they succeeded in becoming the first people in the world to launch an airplane into flight.

It was in Kitty Hawk, North Carolina, over the Kill Devil Hills.

These sandy dunes were so named because, it was said, there was once enough rum buried beneath them to kill the devil. The Wright Flyer sailed through the air above them on its fourth attempt, and in the end succeeded in flying 852 feet in 59 seconds.

Chopsticks and rice were now set out on the table. The fish we were having that day was, ironically enough, flying fish. My mother brandished her chopsticks in her hand but didn't use them to put anything in her mouth, as she was still consumed with telling us about her research.

Crunching down on the dorsal fin of my fried flying fish, I listened to my mother and thought childishly to myself, *Who cares about all this stuff? Everyone can fly now! The miso soup Dad made is getting cold, you should stop talking and concentrate on that.*

"The wind is awful today, huh? Damn headwinds."

Makino said this to me as he adjusted his gold-rimmed glasses, having just sneezed. "Even if we beat our wings as hard as we can, we'll still be late for the morning assembly!"

I gave him a perfunctory answer and tried to concentrate on flying, but Makino persisted, pursuing me through the sky.

"That street down there," he said, drawing me up short by tugging on my wing and pointing to the ground beneath us. He closed one eye and made a show of tracing the road's path with his finger in the air.

He continued, a bit haughtily.

"I heard that's where the Tobita sisters are going."

It was the road that ran straight through town. The road to the sea.

I wasn't intending to look down at it, but thanks to Makino, I found myself following it with my eyes. How many kilometers was it? It would take less than ten minutes to fly, of course.

The sun's rays shone down on the asphalt, making it glint silver here and there along its length.

"I know," I replied, snorting a bit derisively. "Everyone does. Now, let's get going before we're really late!"

I playfully bumped Makino's wing with mine, then took off as fast as my wings could carry me, riding the wind without a backward glance.

◊

It only took a comparative blink of an eye before the Wright brothers' 1903 flying machine was developed for practical use. In the span of eleven years, swarms of planes filled the skies over Europe during World War I. And during World War II, the skies over the whole world buzzed with war planes, and not long after its end, the V2 rocket was developed, which could fly into space.

Subsequently, the Soviet Union launched first Sputnik 2, carrying the space dog Laika, and then Vostok 1, carrying the human cosmonaut Yuri Gagarin, into space. In this way, our ancestors conquered first the skies, then space, then finally stepped foot on the surface of the moon.

During this period, France conducted many experiments launching cats into space; during one such experiment, the cat managed to run away just before the flight was to occur. The cat was never found, and it is in honor of this brave runaway that our Felix was named.

◈

Makino wasn't the only one who gossiped about the Tobita sisters—everyone did.

First of all, they were beautiful. It would be no overstatement to call them the most beautiful in our class, our year, even the whole city. Deep hawk-brown eyes; long, blue-black hair, lustrous as a swallow's back; lips the color of cardinals. Their pure white wings were full and airy as they spread expansively from their backs. They turned the heads of men and women alike wherever they went—people found it hard to get them out of their heads.

But at the same time, they were also quite peculiar.

Rumors swirled about their background—that their father had been taken to a psychiatric institution after he tried to cut off his own wings, or that their mother's ancestors had been legendary marathon runners. Perhaps in tribute to the latter, or for some other mysterious reason, the sisters always wore little sneakers on their feet.

A mystifying custom.

I couldn't remember ever wearing a shoe.

After all, the things were rather a hindrance during flight. It was a big deal if you lost a shoe into the valleys between the buildings, and there had been incidents when a shoelace tangled in an electric line, resulting in death. Shoes were obsolete relics of times past, like corsets. They could be beautiful, of course—high heels made of glass; dress shoes made of supple, polished calfskin; sandals decorated with real diamonds—but as antiques for display, not things to wear. And besides, our feet had grown small and slender with the generations, hardly the kind of appendage suitable for a shoe.

So it was a shock when the Tobita sisters showed up for school decked out in matching neon-blue-and-yellow sneakers. The sight of them dangling at the ends of the long, thin legs of the sisters in their miniskirts made for a strange counterpoint to the expanse of their wings.

❦

The Concorde—a passenger airliner with a name meaning *harmony* that could fly at supersonic speeds—appeared, then disappeared. But only slightly slower passenger planes became incredibly common, and our ancestors spent countless hours of their lives flying around in them. Networks of airways spread across the globe, and by the 2000s, more than 90,000 planes would crisscross the skies every day. Though not everyone could fly in those days—it was primarily people from the developed world, plus the wealthy elite from the developing. But the spread of air travel coincided with the development of telephone communication and eventually the internet, resulting a world that our ancestors felt was getting smaller and more crowded, trapping them in the feeling that everything there was to know and everywhere there was to go had already been discovered.

It was starting then that we began to lift off the ground ourselves, I think.

And after that, it wasn't long before the first wings began to sprout from people's backs.

They were small at first, of course, but steadily became larger and larger.

Like people in places like India spending their food budget to keep their cell phones running, people began to covet wings more than anything, willing to sacrifice any necessity. But soon, wings began to sprout on those from all walks of life, and people who would have never ridden in an airplane in their lives became able to fly.

◊

It was going to start at four o'clock, right after school.

Makino informed me of this as he ate his sweet melon bread, casting a look my way that said of course we were going to go and watch together. I concentrated on stuffing my own melon bread into my mouth, ignoring him.

What was to start at four was the Tobita sisters' run down the road to the sea.

The Tobita sisters were going to . . . run.

Run along the ground.

However many kilometers to the sea, the sisters intended to stay with their feet on the ground the whole time, running.

Our ancestors would fall over dead if they heard that, I thought, though on second thought, they were already dead, so I guess their souls would rise up to smite us. They'd worked so hard to finally achieve flight at the expense of life and limb over hundreds of years, and now these girls were going to start crawling along the ground again on purpose?

The cat that lived behind the school came over as we ate, and I broke off a piece of my melon bread to share with it. The cat flipped over to show its belly to me and purred, grinding its wingless striped back into the dirt as it squirmed around. I reached my hand down to stroke its belly, and it leapt up and fled, fast as a bird. I watched the runaway feline as it kicked up leaves on its dash through the camellia and azalea bushes, unable to look away until it disappeared from sight.

It's been half a year since my mother moved out, taking Felix the tortoiseshell cat with her. What would she say if I told her about the Tobita sisters? Knowing her, she'd probably approve.

We finished our melon breads and tried to slip in unnoticed through the windows in the back of the classroom, but a strong wind slipped in with us, and the teacher naturally saw us and made us fly into the hallway and think about what we'd done.

♠

Just as dinosaurs and Neanderthals eventually disappeared from the world, so too did those without wings, who couldn't fly. Though it took a lot less time for this to happen that it had primates walking on all fours to be replaced by humans walking upright on two feet.

Artificial legs and wheelchairs and crutches all disappeared, and nets hung in the air became the menaces that landmines once were; tap dancing was replaced with a vogue for midair ballet. Airways became regulated like sidewalks and roads once were, getting hit by helicopters and airplanes replacing concerns about cars. Where once the focus was on preventing pedestrians from being run over, new rules were put in place to prevent individual flyers from being knocked out of the sky.

So eventually we left our feet behind. No need to run when you can fly.

♠

After my mother left, my father continued to busy himself in the kitchen making miso soup to go with dinner for us to eat, now just the two of us, every night. I never complained.

I couldn't bring myself to ask him, but I was sure that Mom had taken up with another man. She should have tried as hard to understand my father's feeling as she had tried to understand the feelings of ancient wingless people as they strove to fly, I thought, but I left this unsaid as well.

We can fly now, after all. We can go wherever we want. The internet, too, has developed faster than anyone anticipated, so we can easily contact anyone in the world whenever we want, instantly.

Yet we never see our mother anymore, never even receive a single email from her.

I toss and turn in bed. My wings are a bit of hindrance, and I can only sleep on my right side or my left. I close my wings as tightly as I can to my body and raise my tiny, unreliable feet off the bed to look at them.

Otto Lilienthal or the Wright brothers would surely never have understood how I felt in that moment.

◈

The pollen and dust in the air had cleared, and the wind had stopped.

Though what kind of wind is best for running, anyway?

My mother told me that once, long, long ago, our ancestors had been watching with their own eyes as a shuttle was launched into space. The shuttle took off from the Kennedy Space Center in Florida; its name was Discovery. A huge crowd of people had gathered, beer in hand, in the Space Park to watch.

The shuttle, as they watched it arc above them, became engulfed in light, trailing a long, pure white tail through the sky. Our ancestors were so moved by the sight, my mother told me, that they made sketches of it that were passed down through the generations all the way to today.

Our ancestors were always looking up at the sky. They wanted to discover what was out there, beyond where they currently were, beyond where the eye could see.

Makino wrote a note on a piece of paper, then folded it into an airplane and threw it at me.

It hit me on the wing and fell onto the desk in front of me. I unfolded it.

What are you betting?

Betting? I turned and mouthed my question to him, to which I received another paper airplane in reply. I caught this one. When I unfolded it, I saw the answer scrawled across the paper in pencil.

If the Tobitas make it all the way to the sea, you owe me a year's worth of milk coffee!

So the bet was whether the Tobita sisters would really run the whole length of the road, all the way to the water.

It seemed obvious that they wouldn't, not on what are surely tiny, shrunken feet never made to touch the ground. Sure, they might be able to walk a few steps, but they weren't ostriches! Birds that fly don't run for kilometers at a time. Worst case, they might hurt themselves, even die! Though the Tobita sisters were a special case—they were surely practicing every morning, building the strength of their feet and legs. Everyone was debating the likelihood of their success, and soon everyone was getting in on the action, too—betting candy and allowance money, promises to pull their pants down in front of everyone or buy each other high-priced concert tickets.

I crumpled up the unfolded paper airplane in my hand and shoved it in my pocket.

So stupid!

I felt restless, like I couldn't decide whether to sit down or stand up. Though I guess it's hard for us to really "stand up," but you know what I mean.

It didn't matter to me one way or the other if the Tobita sisters in their weird, bright-colored sneakers managed to crawl along the ground all the way to the water. *If they wanted to go to the sea so bad*, I thought, *they could just fly!*

Outside the classroom windows, I could see students rising up into the air. Girls' miniskirts flapped in the breeze as they flew up into the bright, pale sky, their long, thin legs and tiny feet dangling below them. I watched as they ascended.

They were all headed toward the sea, so they could see for themselves if the Tobita sisters would achieve their goal.

Our teacher didn't seem to even notice the exodus outside, hovering in the air in front of the blackboard as he explained the mechanics of butterfly wings.

Our ancestors used to talk about something they called the butterfly effect—the idea that the flap of a butterfly's wing in Beijing could cause a chain of events leading to a hurricane in New York. This was used to explain chaos theory at the time, but these days, as you know, we've developed the tools to accurately predict the course of events so precisely that we can actually trace a butterfly's wingbeat to the hurricane it causes on the other side of the world.

I was already standing up from my desk as he spoke, and I

went to the window in the back, opened it, and placed my feet on the sill.

And then, I flew.

The wind had died, so the teacher didn't notice me slipping out the window this time. Looking back, I could see that only Makino seemed to have noticed, shoving his textbook and cell phone in his bag as flipped me off and yelled after me, *Oi! Come back here, don't leave me behind!*

I drifted a little and found the wind. I spread my wings and caught the updraft, riding it as it propelled me swiftly into the air.

I flew across the sky.

I looked down at the school, the houses, the city streets.

I rode the wind. My hair, my tie, the cord of the earphones pumping music into my ears—all fluttered as I flew.

I saw the road that headed straight through the city to the sea.

I closed one eye and held my finger out, tracings its path in the air.

I flew. The opposite direction everyone else was flying.

♠

It was four o'clock.

The Tobita sisters were slowly folding their wings against their bodies as they floated to the ground.

Now, they would begin to run.

Everyone was watching, each with their own stakes in the outcome. Both cheers and derision rained down on them from the sky.

Where are you?

Makino was sending me text after text.

It's about to start!

&

I was all alone, hovering in the sky above a hill outside town.

I was slowly folding my wings against my body as I floated to the ground.

The cold asphalt came into contact with my toes, then the bottoms of my feet, ending with my heels as I touched down.

Finally, I folded my wings all the way and felt the full force of gravity, and it knocked me off my feet. I stuck my arms out as I fell.

The cold asphalt came into contact with the palms of my hands.

And then, slowly, I stood back up.

It had only been a second.

I was still wobbly, but I was standing, holding myself up with both feet on the ground.

I took a step.

I lost my balance again, and my body threatened to topple once more to the ground.

At some point, if I ever have the chance to talk to the Tobita sisters, I'll have to ask them.

Where can I find a pair of sneakers like theirs, that would fit so perfectly on my feet?

That would fit so perfectly on my feet, and look so crazy dangling from my body?

I saw a cat dash across the road and run away, so fast.
If my mother were to come back one day, I'd tell her, I thought.
Slowly, with my tiny feet, I pushed against the ground.
The sun began to set.
The wind began to get colder.
I'd tell her what it was like, right here, right now, as I began to run.

HIS LAST BOW

"I fear that Mr. Sherlock Holmes may become like one of those popular tenors who, having outlived their time, are still tempted to make repeated farewell bows to their indulgent audiences. This must cease and he must go the way of all flesh, material or imaginary."

Sir Conan Doyle, *The Case-Book of Sherlock Holmes* (1927)

HE HOLDS HIS just-born son to his chest. Swaddled in white cloth, his son breathes softly, his tiny nostrils flaring slightly as air passes through them. His newborn skin is still covered in golden fuzz, and the world reflected in his dark, depthless eyes is just a faint haze. They are eyes not yet able to meet his father's. Instead, they slowly close as he lies there in his father's slightly sweaty arms. A faint unease pricks the father, unbidden—did this tiny existence just wink out entirely? As town doctor, he's witnessed countless souls passing on from this world; it's much rarer to see one entering it.

He knows his son, when he grows up, will more than likely become a doctor too. After all, his own father had been one, and his father's father, and his father before that: generations of doctors leading up to the present. There's even a golden figure of Yakushi Nyorai, the Medicine Buddha, glittering in a small shrine in the garden—how long ago had it been placed there? The dark green foliage of fig trees spreads above it. Would his son become a surgeon or a general practitioner? Whichever the case, the birth of a son to follow in his footsteps was cause for celebration. Soon the red rice would be made and distributed to the neighbors. This son of countless generations of doctors received the name Shigeru. It was 1898, the thirty-first year of Meiji.

It was one year later that a translation of the first Sherlock Holmes story, "A Study in Scarlet," was serialized in a Japanese newspaper. And only two years prior, Wilhelm Conrad Röntgen had presented his discovery of the mysterious radiation he named after the mathematical symbol of the unknown: X.

The word *radioactive* itself had only recently been coined.

The child's cry rings out. Pure white steam rises from the boiling water and disappears.

The predictions the father made as he held his newborn son all come true: red rice is distributed to the neighbors; little Shigeru grows up to be a doctor. Shigeru enters medical school in Kanagawa on a scholarship from the army, going on to become a student at the military medical school and then at Kanazawa Medical University, specializing in diagnostic sciences, eventually becoming an army doctor attached to the military hospital in Hirosaki.

His specialty turns out to be neither surgery or internal medicine, but rather the form of radiation discovered by Röntgen around the time he was born: the X-ray.

Shigeru attempts to see that which cannot be seen.

Invisible light penetrates human flesh. Things that could never before be seen become visible, burned onto photographic plates.

Shigeru is my grandfather.

He died when I was still in my mother's womb, so I've only ever seen him in photographs.

According to those who knew him, he was a strict and meticulous man. He would disinfect the skins of apples with rubbing alcohol. His favorite fruit was figs—did he happily eat the insects that lie within them?

Our ancestral home near Gamagori, in Aichi, was one that he built. It was an old wooden house carpeted in green. The shining Medicine Buddha figure in its shrine lay a few minutes away by car. There was a little restaurant near it known for its huge fried shrimp. Bottles of Mitsuya Cider were always stacked by the case in the kitchen where my grandmother, who suffered from diabetes, cooked. I would look up at the black-and-white photograph of my grandfather that hung in the living room. His aquiline nose. His almond-shaped eyes. The tidy mustache above his lip.

Did I look like him?

Something stirred faintly in my chest.

He holds his just-born son to his chest. Swaddled in white cloth, his son's lips tighten, giving him a perturbed look. His thin skin grows redder and redder, and the world reflected in his deep,

dark eyes only barely seems to register. They are eyes not yet able
to meet his father's. Held in his father's frozen arms, the son
begins to cry. The father is momentarily gripped with unease—
will this little life be snuffed out so soon? The father uses the
Eastman Kodak camera he bought back in his Kanazawa Medical School days to take a picture of his son.

He knows his son, when he grows up, will more than likely
become a doctor too. After all, his own father had been one, and
his father's father, and his father before that: this is a family
made up of generations of doctors.

The garden behind the house is covered in snow—nothing is
visible.

But even without the snow, the Medicine Buddha would be
nowhere to be seen. He's living far from the town where he grew
up, in Hirosaki, up in Aomori. He'd become a level-one army
doctor, running the X-ray Department at the Hirosaki Military
Hospital. His graduate thesis was titled, "X-ray Research into
Soldiers' Hearts."

Everything around him now is white.

The snow is bound to continue for some time yet.

Would his son become a surgeon? A general practitioner? An
X-ray specialist? Whichever the case, the birth of a son to follow
in his footsteps was cause for celebration. Soon the red rice would
be made and distributed to the neighbors. This son of countless
generations of doctors received the name Tsukasa. It was 1929,
the fourth year of Showa.

Two years prior, in England, Sir Arthur Conan Doyle had
announced the end of the Sherlock Holmes series, which he'd
been writing for the past forty-one years. That same year, Wer-

ner Karl Heisenberg, who would go on to contribute to the development of nuclear weapons in Nazi Germany, published his paper on the uncertainty principle.

A great horror was beginning to spread across the world.

The child's cry rings out. Pure white steam rises from the boiling water and disappears.

The predictions the father made as he held his newborn son turn out to be half-correct and half-mistaken.

Tsukasa is my father.

He was born in Hirosaki, up in Aomori, but he was raised in Harbin, Manchuria. His father ascended in rank to become a level-three army doctor, assigned to work with the 11th Air Squadron stationed in Harbin. One year after the Pacific War began, he moved back to Kanazawa to become the head of the military hospital there.

Before long, though, he turned in his resignation, clasped his hands in prayer before the Medicine Buddha, and joined the 17th Division as an army doctor, traveling with them to Rabaul, on the island of New Britain.

The war continued and my father grew up, passing the admittance test for the Kanazawa Fourth School, preparing his way to becoming a doctor. But just as he passed it, the government assigned him to work in an airplane factory in the city of Inami, in Toyama. He installed engines into army-type reconnaissance planes.

Then, before he had a chance to become a doctor, two nuclear bombs were dropped on Japan.

On August 6, a uranium bomb called Little Boy was dropped on Hiroshima.

On August 9, a plutonium bomb called Fat Man was dropped on Nagasaki.

My father took a page out of the newspaper and wrote in ink on its back side.

August 10. Clear skies. Brave students, join the kamikaze forces— bodies on the front lines! Today was a beautiful day.

Invisible light penetrates human flesh. Bodies are incinerated in an instant, their shadows burned into concrete.

Japan is defeated. Nonetheless, my father continues his studies to become a doctor. His father returns to Japan a year and a half after the war's end. He is no longer a military doctor. He borrows money from his relatives and opens a modest practice in Gamagori, back in Aichi. It's not far from where the golden Medicine Buddha stands in his little shrine. He becomes the town doctor, just as his father's father had been.

My father graduates from the Fourth School, then from the Niigata University School of Medicine, and then joins the University of Tokyo Faculty of Medicine's neuropsychiatry department. He receives a Fulbright scholarship and boards the *Hikawa-maru* ocean liner to America, working as a researcher at the University of Pittsburgh Psychiatric Research Center and then the Galesburg State Research Hospital. He returns to Japan and begins to work in Tokyo, at the Psychiatric Research Center at Seiwa Hospital.

So—he has become a doctor.

But not a surgeon, nor a general practitioner, nor an X-ray specialist. His specialty is psychopharmacology.

He tries to see things that cannot be seen.

In this way, he may resemble his ancestors.

Except that, after fathering three daughters and just before fathering his fourth—that is, me—he quits medicine entirely.

My father was someone who hated to clean up. He left his books around, he didn't wash properly in the bath, he never cleaned the wax from his ears. The old house in Tokyo's Nerima district that he rented when he returned from America was always dirty, but neither my mother nor me nor my sisters lifted a finger to clean it. For we'd learned that if we took it upon ourselves to do so, he'd get angry.

When I was young, I'd lay on the camellia-patterned futon I shared with my three sisters and while away the time watching dust play in the light streaming in through the window.

I could hear my mother and father talking in the kitchen.

They discussed murders in Victorian England, shooting up cocaine in opium dens, scandal after scandal.

It was all they ever seemed to talk about.

For my father had become a Sherlock Holmes scholar.

By the time I'd grown up, my mother and father had co-translated all sixty works featuring Sherlock Holmes into Japanese.

My father died the year before the Great East Japan Earthquake in 2011.

Eighty years had passed by then since the death of Sherlock Holmes's creator, Sir Arthur Conan Doyle.

One hundred and twelve years had passed since the coining of the word *radioactive*.

My father left us before knowing of the accident at Fukushima

Daiichi nuclear power plant, before knowing that radioactive material would fall down upon us, before knowing that I would give birth to a child.

◈

He holds the just-born child to his chest. I watch as he holds the child. Swaddled in white cloth, the child cries out in high-pitched squeals again and again. Waxy pieces of vernix still dot the newborn skin, and the world reflected in the child's dark, depthless eyes is just a faint haze. They are eyes not yet able to meet another's. Resting in his hands there in the pastel-painted waiting room, the child suddenly grows quiet. He is momentarily gripped with unease—did this tiny life just wink out entirely? He is not a doctor and this is the first time he's seen a person newly born.

Will he change, once the child grows up?

He doesn't even know for sure the child is his.

In the corner of the waiting room, a woman holds her child to her chest, murmuring as if singing a song.

Through the window, all that is visible are buildings and a construction site.

The red rice will be bought by my mother at a grocery store the day after I leave the hospital. In our small Tokyo apartment, we have no one to distribute it to, and we end up eating it all ourselves.

The child, nestled in a cradle in the living room and wrapped in a towel, blinks slowly.

Something stirs faintly in my chest.

Does this child resemble him?

Does this child resemble him, or any of them?

I did not become a doctor; I became a writer. The youngest of four sisters, I am the twelfth generation, and the house of my father and all the fathers before him is now gone. They all had been doctors, but I heal no one. Last year, the figure of the Medicine Buddha and the small shrine it stood in were moved to another shrine. The fig trees are also gone—whether they died or were cut down, I don't know.

The child's cry rings out. Pure white steam rises from the boiling water and disappears.

Invisible light penetrates human flesh. All the things that could not be seen are now revealed, right before my eyes.

THE FOREST OF
WILD BIRDS

THIS USED TO be a place called the Forest of Wild Birds.

Of course, that wasn't its official name—it was just what everyone in the area, including the people at Tokyo Electric, called it. A grand forest once grew here, and you could hear birdsong day and night.

Several times a year, they would open the area to the public, and families would come and enjoy themselves. They would spread blue tarps on the grass and stare up at the mountain cherries in full bloom. People would braid flowering white clover into crowns to place on their children's heads.

THE FOREST OF WILD BIRDS

This place is also the Tokyo Electric Power Company's Fukushima Daiichi Nuclear Power Plant, known in the industry as 1F.

Its grounds are extensive, and they say they once overflowed with green.

◊

In the spring of 2017, I took Route 6 north from Iwaki Station to visit the TEPCO Fukushima Daiichi Nuclear Power Plant. It was April—the government had just recently declared part of the city of Tomioka to no longer be a nuclear exclusion zone. The launching point for tours of the nuclear power plant had long been the J-Village athletic center, which, following the Fukushima disaster, had been used as a relay point for those working to clean it up. But ever since Tokyo was chosen as the site for the next Olympics, J-Village had been undergoing hurried reconstruction so it could be used again for athletics (this led eventually to it being made the Olympic torch relay starting point).

So instead, I was heading toward the former "Energy Museum" at the TEPCO Fukushima Daini Nuclear Power Plant (2F). It juts at a sudden angle to a shopping mall with a sign advertising ATOMIC SUSHI. The museum is like a fantasy of Western architecture, a set of three conjoined buildings painted in pastels that wouldn't be out of place in Disneyland. Asking about it, I learned that the three buildings were modeled after the homes of Albert Einstein, Marie Curie, and Thomas Edison. These days, it has been reopened as a Decommissioning Archive Center, and the public can visit it whenever they wish. Admission is free.

I was guided into the closed Energy Museum for the orientation before the power plant tour. Entering a room at the end of the hall, I was confronted with walls still decorated with anime-inspired images. I learned about the decommissioning process and what to pay attention to during the tour of the power plant while surrounded by storybook images of blooming flowers and freshly baked bread.

Cameras and cell phones were strictly prohibited—only pen, paper, and a radiation dosimeter were permitted. We all climbed into a small van with plastic-covered seats and headed toward the power plant grounds.

⋔

The 3/11 Great East Japan Earthquake and the ensuing nuclear disaster at TEPCO's Fukushima Daiichi Nuclear Power Plant—I remember the images I saw on the news: debris, ruined buildings, and, as if to cover over the wreckage, encroaching vegetation. Wild animals and animals left behind by evacuated residents roamed the abandoned streets, including cows who'd escaped their farms, dogs and cats left behind by their owners, and wild boars taking up residence in people's homes. Any humans I saw were dressed head-to-toe in pure white hazmat suits.

In other words, the "Fukushima" in my head was an irradiated landscape, irrevocably contaminated. But during the tour I never had to change into a hazmat suit even once. I didn't even have to wear a mask. And the landscape that greeted me at the famous Daiichi Nuclear Power Plant, far from being overgrown with vegetation, was a sci-fi expanse of smooth, silvery cement as far as the eye could see.

We passed through several gates and checkpoints and eventually arrived inside the facility's grounds. We were brought into a prefab building there. It was an enormous service area, nine floors high and able to accommodate up to 1,200 people at a time. Men working at the nuclear plant passed through a checkpoint that was a radiation dosimeter as they came and went. It was so clean and brightly lit, it reminded me of a convenience store—and in fact, there was a convenience store in it. A Lawson. I was told it had just opened for business.

I gazed at the illuminated blue-and-white sign. It was exactly like the one in my own neighborhood back in Tokyo.

From the building, we were driven (in a different van—though the seats were covered in plastic in this one too) around the grounds to view the facility. Looking out the van windows, all I saw was a single, uninterrupted silver surface. When I asked about it, I was informed that falling radiation stuck to the grass and trees and raised the ambient radiation levels, and when rain would fall, it would pick up radiation from the vegetation and soil and further pollute the water, so all the trees were cut down and all the grass and soil covered with cement. The felled trees were high in radiation themselves, so they were being stored in a separate place elsewhere on the grounds. The soil had been sealed over just as it was, its undulating surface frozen in soft waves. Looking at this silver landscape spreading out in all directions, it struck me as even a bit beautiful.

The van continued its slow drive through the facility, and soon enough we were passing by the first tower, its walls and roof still blown off. There were lines of cranes surrounding it, and we could see the figures of decommissioning workers passing back and forth. From time to time we passed digital signs displaying radiation levels. The levels near the second and third towers were still high, but elsewhere, perhaps thanks to the cement covering the ground, the levels were relatively low. My only protective gear was a pair of cotton gloves they had me wear, presumably so that in the unlikely event I came in contact with radioactive material, it would stick to the gloves rather than directly to my skin. An APD—area passive dosimeter—hung around my neck.

When we returned to the large prefab building, we ate lunch in the cafeteria inside. Fifty to sixty workers were eating there with us. They were all men, many young, some with their hair modishly dyed brown or blond. The lunch menu featured five choices: two types of set meal, a rice bowl, a noodle dish, and a curry. All were just ¥380. I chose the fried chicken set meal with grated daikon and deep-fried tofu with vegetables. It was delicious. The lunches were delivered from the Fukushima Revitalization Meal Service Center in the nearby city of Ōkuma. And in fact, we ended up touring that facility too. Unlike at the nuclear facility, there were many women working there. The facility allowed for rice to be prepared and cooked at the touch of a button, and it was able to make enough for around 3,000 meals at once. The fruit and vegetables were all Fukushima-grown. We were told that the menu was never the same two days in a month.

After lunch, I took the elevator up to the top floor. Looking out from a circular window, I contemplated the rows of huge blue-and-white tanks that stretched all the way to the sea.

This was the former site of the Forest of Wild Birds. The Tokyo Electric employee leading the tour was the one who told us about the former forest. Now, instead of trees, the site is covered with tanks of contaminated water. A single row of cherry trees remained, a line of vivid pink amid the tanks.

Hadn't I been trying to think of "Fukushima"—this irradiated, contaminated place—as somewhere completely separate, a place with nothing in common with where I lived?

This invisible thing called "radiation."

Hadn't I even been comforted when I looked at the images of debris and ruin left by the disaster, as it seemed they made radiation visible, tangible?

But now, looking at Fukushima as it really was, I could no longer deny that it was utterly continuous with the world in which I made my home too.

During World War II, this former landscape—the Forest of Wild Birds—had been the Iwaki Airfield used by the Kumagaya Military Air Force School. In other words, it had been a training grounds for kamikaze pilots.

I wanted to know the names of the plants that used to grow here. I submitted my request and, after a bit of a wait, received my answer. Four or five years before the nuclear accident, a survey of the area had been conducted and the resulting environmental impact assessment submitted to the Ministry of the Environment.

Common fleabane, cat's-ear, lovegrass, cudweed, Japanese clover, pampas grass, mugwort, fever vine, gooseneck loosestrife, red pine, mountain clover, cat-clover, horsetail, Chinese clover, sparrow's woodrush, shady clubmoss, goldenrod, bloodgrass, wild soybean, mare's tail, crabgrass, daisy fleabane, white clover . . .

The place I initially wrote to for information answered dismissively, writing that paperwork from that time was almost entirely lost and that now, nearly six years after the accident, people able to provide first-hand accounts were almost unfindable, so it would take a prohibitive amount of time to conduct further research into the lost Forest of Wild Birds. So, I filed an information disclosure request directly to the Ministry of Environment myself and received the assessment results. The list of vegetation was much more detailed.

Jolcham oak, aohada, Korean hill cherry, chestnut, fir, torch azalea, Japanese sumac, Japanese snowbell, spindle tree, oriental photinia, Japanese pieris, variegated dwarf bamboo, China root, marlberry, Japanese fairybell, noble orchid, pickerel weed, water plantain, marsh dewflower, swamp millet, kasasuge grass, Maui sedge, streambank bulrush . . .

🔥

I go over the names one by one.

And as I do, I wonder how distinctly I can imagine each plant—each grass, each flower.

After all, spring is coming, once again.

TRANSLATOR'S AFTERWORD

My first encounter with Erika Kobayashi occurred in 2015, during a conference organized by Livia Monnet at the Université de Montréal called Rethinking Radiation Ecologies. Kobayashi had just published her debut novel, *Breakfast with Madame Curie* (*Madamu kyurii to chōshoku o*, Shūeisha, 2014), to much acclaim in Japan, and she discussed this novel and her similarly themed manga, *Children of Light: LUMINOUS* (*Hikari no kodomo*, Little More, 2013). I was struck at the time by the clarity and poise of her work—its poetic, lambent beauty—even as it explored such potentially heavy themes as radiation, histories of fascism in Japan and elsewhere, and death at both intensely personal and grandly global scales. We kept in touch after the conference, which lead to the opportunity for me to translate "Sunrise," the first piece included in this collection, which was presented as part of the similarly titled art installation included in the *My Body, Your Voice* group exhibition at the Mori Art Museum in 2016.

Like many of the shorter works in this collection, the text of "Sunrise" was distributed to gallery visitors in both Japanese and English as they entered a carefully constructed space filled with resonant objects. One of the objects in this space was a circle of braided red yarn mounted on the gallery wall. This simple piece gains symbolic power after reading that the red yarn was part of an unfinished knitting project left behind by Kobayashi's grandmother when she passed away the same year that an earthquake and tsunami struck northeastern Japan and caused the catastrophic accident at the Fukushima Daiichi Nuclear Power Plant. Kobayashi took over her grandmother's work, using the leftover yarn to knit a circle the exact circumference of the Gadget—the world's first nuclear bomb, detonated at the Trinity testing site in New Mexico in 1945. Looking at the perfect red circle mounted on the wall, it is also impossible not to be reminded of the red circle in the center of the Japanese flag, which, in Japanese, is called the hi no maru—literally, the *circle of the sun*. Erika Kobayashi condenses personal, national, and world history into a single object, humble in its simplicity even as it shimmers with the world-exploding energy of the bomb it evokes in its dimensions.

I am exploring this piece in detail because I think it exemplifies Kobayashi's method not just when creating mixed media works for gallery spaces, but when assembling her purely prose pieces as well. Short pieces like "Sunrise" work both in their original gallery context and outside it, on their own terms, because the compressed resonance of Kobayashi's layering of the intimate and personal with the grandly world-historical can be felt in the layers of lines comprising the writing itself. "Sunrise" begins with an evocation of the almost impossible-to-comprehend dimensions of the literal sun before evoking the all-too-easily comprehensible physical dimensions of a nuclear bomb waiting to be detonated, then gracefully layers the arc of Japanese postwar history and its increasing entanglement with the development of nuclear power over the arc of her mother's life navigating that history as an individual woman. These deft shifts in scale and perspective are some of the most consistent and powerful features of Kobayashi's writing, not just in these short pieces but across her fiction as a whole.

Kobayashi's overarching concern is with evoking "that which cannot be seen," as she has put it numerous times in interviews when discussing her work. Literature, for her, is a way to make the invisible visible. Radiation, of course, is prime among these invisible phenomena, but it is not the only one she explores in her work. In her novel

Trinity, Trinity, Trinity, published in Japanese in 2019 (and made available in English from Astra House in 2022), radiation becomes visible in the actions and words of those afflicted from the Trinity disease, but the book evokes other unseen forces animating our daily lives as well, including electronic economic transactions conducted by credit cards and train passes, remote controls communicating with televisions, and individual movements tracked by phones and tablets. The stories in this collection, which include some written in the lead-up to *Trinity, Trinity, Trinity*, as well as many written after its release, explore the world as a matrix of unseen forces in much the same way. In "Precious Stones," for example, the titular stones knit together episodes in the narrator's life and the life of her grandmother, whom she never met, their crystalline condensation of time acting as a kind of kaleidoscopic lens through which histories both personal and world-historic refract and illuminate each other. In "Shedding," the other novella-length work included in this collection, the unseen force of radiation is replaced by that of a mysterious virus whose presence manifests as a series of fault lines opening up along the similarly unseen networks of communication represented by language. As patients lose their ability to communicate and remember, the world around them uses language to dehumanize and then banish them. Written and published in 2020, during the height of COVID-19 quarantine in Japan, the story's meditations on the nature of knowing and communicating in an age of forgetting and ostracism ring all the truer in the so-called post-pandemic world of today.

Intergenerational moments of communication and miscommunication (or even communication *through* miscommunication) inform Kobayashi's speculative pieces that, on the surface, avoid her usual concern with nuclear radiation. A grandmother's words (and forbidden sweets) resonate throughout the treeless future of "A Tale of Burning Books," while "The Flying Tobita Sisters" ends with the protagonist's wish to communicate his experience of running along the ground again to his absent mother. And in the story "See," a drug that temporarily blinds its users paradoxically allows a daughter to understand her mother at last, to the point that the difference between the two begins to blur completely. In an interview published at the time of its publication, Kobayashi explains that she wrote "See" while pregnant with her first child, a daughter. She says that the impetus for the story was her realization that she, as a daughter, was unable to know her mother as a woman outside her capacity as mother, and that her own daughter would have the same relation to her. The story's witty use of a drug that robs its main character of visual perception to enhance that same character's perception of aspects of her mother previously invisible to her exemplifies Kobayashi's literary and artistic method in general: the creation of flashes of illumination out of moments of unknowing and darkness.

The dominant narratives of Japanese and world history are, of course, filled with aporias, consigning the perceptions and experiences of many to the dark margins of that history, particularly women and other minorities. By making her stories of interpersonal and intergenerational communication and miscommunication resonate so forcefully with under-recognized or even suppressed aspects of history—the race to develop a Japanese nuclear bomb during World War II, the tangled history of the Olympics and fascism, the inextricability of Japan's investment in nuclear power from the story of its postwar economic recovery—Kobayashi renders the invisible forces animating the world perceptible even in their invisibility.

This makes Kobayashi's work resonate very personally for me, as well, as someone who grew up in rural eastern Washington, a region that also features the Hanford Site, which was established in 1943 and produced plutonium that was used in the Gadget and later in Fat Man, the atomic bomb that was dropped on Nagasaki. I grew up in

the 1980s and '90s seeing the occasional local news report on the is-
sues related to downwinders, the name given to the people, mainly
farmers, who lived downwind from the site and were petitioning the
government for recognition of the various health problems in these
communities that appeared to be linked to radioactive contamination.
Besides the occasional investigative report in local newspapers like
Spokane's *Spokesman Review*, the only people who seemed to be pay-
ing attention to the issue in the face of government denials of causal
links between the Hanford Site and the downwinders' health problems were the Japanese. The documentary filmmaker Hitomi Ka-
manaka devotes a third of her 2003 movie *Hibakusha at the End of the
World* to the issue, and downwinders' first-person testimonies have been
exhibited at the Hiroshima Peace Memorial Museum. On a more personal note, I recall my grandmother telling me excitedly that a Japanese
documentary film crew had filmed an interview with her hairdresser
while the hairdresser was cutting her hair ("The back of my head will
be on Japanese TV!"); her hairdresser was a downwinder whose
daughter, now a music teacher, had been born without eyes.

As I grew up, the stories of the downwinders were an ominous
presence at the edges of public consciousness—like the radiation that
affected them, these victims of the nuclear age were largely unper-
ceived, rendered invisible and inaudible in mainstream media. Seeing
the Japanese government arbitrarily raise the allowable levels of background radiation in the aftermath of the triple disaster in Fukushima,
I was reminded of the eerie stonewalling by the government and nuclear industry I'd witnessed growing up, dismissing as unprovable the
links between unprecedented levels of radioactive contamination in
the area and the obvious harm sustained by the people who lived there.
Kobayashi's literary method layers the historical and the personal in a
way that brings these suppressed stories to light, both in her evoca-
tions of less well-known facets of history and in her breaking open of

language itself through her poetic juxtapositions of the individual, the historical, and the mythic.

The photograph used on the cover of this collection is from a series of photos Kobayashi created by lighting her own hand on fire. She borrowed the trick for doing this from the book *Surely You're Joking, Mr. Feynman!*, a collection of lighthearted essays by Richard Feynman, one of the scientists who was part of the Manhattan Project and was present at the detonation of the Gadget at the Trinity Site in New Mexico. The name of the photograph is *In My Hand – The Fire of Prometheus*, which nudges the viewer toward its mythical implications. The image not only by direct association evokes the myth of Prometheus and its metaphorical connection to the miraculous yet dangerous light and heat he stole from the gods and gave to humankind, but also more immediate associations like the "sacred fire" of the Olympic torch, whose history is shown to be so entangled in the history of fascism and war (including nuclear war) in pieces like "She Waited." Yet it is not simply the layers of allusion that render the image so powerful—it is the simplicity of the gesture as well, the way it illuminates so much in such an unfussy, clear way. Lighting her hand on fire, Kobayashi becomes Prometheus, of course, but also becomes Feynman, performing a parlor-trick version of the much grander gesture he made as a scientist bringing the annihilating power of nuclear war into the world, as well as becoming all of us living in the post-nuclear age, holding in our hands the power of light and heat every time we flip a switch or push the button on a remote control or turn a car key.

In this sense, it is a perfect image for the cover of this collection. For like a handful of flame, they are stories that illuminate. And burn.

Brian Bergstrom
September 2022, Montréal

ACKNOWLEDGMENTS

Thank you to the following venues where stories from this collection were originally published in Japanese:

"Sunrise" as "SUNRISE: Hiizuru" as part of the exhibition *Roppongi Crossing 2016: My Body, Your Voice* (Mori Art Museum, 2016); reprinted in *Kanojo wa kagami no naka o nozokikomu* (Tokyo: Shūeisha, 2017)

"A Tale of Burning Books" as "Moeru hon no hanashi" in *Tobu kyōshitsu* (Autumn 2015); reprinted in *Kanojo wa kagami no naka o nozokikomu* (Tokyo: Shūeisha, 2017)

"Precious Stones" as "Hōseki" in *Subaru* (April 2016); reprinted in *Kanojo wa kagami no naka o nozokikomu* (Tokyo: Shūeisha, 2017)

"Hello My Baby, Hello My Honey," as "Konnichiwa, akachan" in *Gunzō* (2021)

"See" as "Shii" in *Waseda bungaku* (Spring 2016); reprinted in *Kanojo wa kagami no naka o nozokikomu* (Tokyo: Shūeisha, 2017)

"Coco's Century" as "100-nen no koko" in *Bijutsu techō* (2019)

"She Waited" as "Kanojo-tachi wa matte ita" as part of the exhibition *Image Narratives: Literature in Japanese Contemporary Art* (The National Art Center Tokyo, 2019)

"Shedding" as "Dappi" in *Gunzō* (2020)

"The Flying Tobita Sisters" as "Tobita shimai no hanashi" in *Hashiru?* (Tokyo: Bunshun bunko, 2017)

"His Last Bow" as "Chichi-tachi no bōken" in *Gunzō* (2019); reprinted in *Bungaku 2020: Nihon bungeika kyōkai-hen shūroku* (Tokyo: Kōdansha, 2020)

ACKNOWLEDGMENTS

The following stories appeared in English, in slightly different form, in the following journals:

"See" in *Asymptote* (Summer 2017)
"Sunrise" in *Asymptote* (Winter 2018)
"Precious Stones" in *Elemental: Earth Stories* (San Francisco: Two Lines Press, 2021)

🔥

The occasion of this book, my second after *Trinity, Trinity, Trinity* in 2022, coming out in English fills me with so much gratitude.

Above all, I must give many thanks to Brian Bergstrom, who reads my work more deeply than anyone else and produces such wonderful translations.

This book wouldn't exist it all if it weren't for the work of another great supporter and reader of my work, my agent, Lisette Verhagen at Peters, Fraser, and Dunlop.

Working once again with the fantastic team at Astra House Books to put together this collection was like a dream, starting with the passionate editing by Rola Harb.

I also want to thank Jeanette Tran and Rodrigo Corral Studio for using my piece *In My Hand – The Fire of Prometheus* (which is a photograph of my own hand, literally on fire) to design a truly miraculous cover for this book.

Thanks as well must be paid to the various editors who shepherded these stories into publication in Japan, including those at Shūeisha, Kōdansha, Bijutsu Shuppan-sha, and Bunshun bunko. Many of the stories in this collection were first presented as parts of exhibitions at galleries and museums, and I am so grateful for the opportunities given to me by Mori Art Museum to be part of the exhibit *Roppongi*

ACKNOWLEDGMENTS

Crossing 2016: My Body, Your Voice, and by the National Art Center, Tokyo to be included in their *Image Narratives: Literature in Japanese Contemporary Art* show, as well as, of course, the primary home for my art, Yutaka Kikutake Gallery in Tokyo. And I would like to take this opportunity to thank Hiroshi Kainuma, who guided me during my trip to the Tokyo Electric Power Company Fukushima Daiichi Nuclear Power Plant following the 2011 Great East Japan Earthquake.

My family, mentors, and friends living in both Japan and in the English-speaking world have done so much to support me as my second book has found publication in English. Thank you.

Soon, the twelfth spring since the accident at the Fukushima Daiichi Nuclear Power Plant will be upon us. It will follow the twelfth winter since my grandmother passed away that same year, an anniversary that will coincide with the seventh birthday of my daughter, who at the time had yet to be born.

And then summer will come, the seventy-eighth since the flash of the world's first nuclear bomb.

I can only wish for us to begin to notice the things around us that cannot be seen, to perceive them even in their invisibility.

Finally, to each and every person who has picked up this book and read its words, I thank you from the bottom of my heart.

Erika Kobayashi
Fall 2022

PHOTO BY MIE MORIMOTO

ABOUT THE AUTHOR

Erika Kobayashi is a novelist and visual artist based in Tokyo. Kobayashi creates works that are inspired by matters invisible to the eye: time and history, family and memory, and the traces often left behind in places. Her novel *Breakfast with Madame Curie* (Shūeisha,) was shortlisted for both the Mishima and the Akutagawa Prize and she was awarded the 44th Japan Sherlock Holmes Club Encouragement Award in 2022 for her novel *His Last Bow* (Kodansha) and the 7th Tekken Heterotopia Literary Prize in 2020 for her novel *Trinity, Trinity, Trinity* (Shūeisha).

Her first novel to be published in English, *Trinity, Trinity, Trinity* (Astra House) also won the the 2022–2023 Japan-U.S. Friendship Commission Prizes (JUSFC) for the English translation of Japanese literature. *Sunrise: Radiant Stories* is her second work of fiction to be published in English.

ABOUT THE TRANSLATOR

Brian Bergstrom is a lecturer and translator who has lived in Chicago, Kyoto, and Yokohama. His writing and translations have appeared in publications including *Granta*, *Aperture*, *Lit Hub*, *Mechademia*, *Japan Forum*, *positions: asia critique*, and *The Penguin Book of Japanese Short Stories*. He is the editor and principal translator of *We, the Children of Cats* by Tomoyuki Hoshino (PM Press), which was longlisted for the 2013 Best Translated Book Award. His translation of *Trinity, Trinity, Trinity* by Erika Kobayashi (Astra House, 2022) won the 2022–2023 Japan-U.S. Friendship Commission (JUSFC) Prize for the Translation of Japanese Literature. He is currently based in Montréal, Canada.